The Hallowed Grove

Andrew Fordham

Thank you for buying my book – I really hope you enjoy reading it. When you have finished and if you have time, could you please leave a review?

You can find out more about my series of books at :

Andrew Fordham : Amazon Author Page

I really enjoy engaging with readers of my books and will be setting up a blog page on my website, where over time, I will give insights into my writing processes - such as characterisation, settings, and plot research, and will also use the Blog pages to keep readers informed of my upcoming new books and series.

I hope to see you there !

Folk Horror Styled Ghost Stories

My stories are a fusion of contemporary folk horror and classic styled ghost tales, inspired by and incorporating elements of myth, folklore, archaeology, the occult, psychogeography, and history.

For me, living in East Anglia, I feel surrounded by the vibes of what I can relate to as 'Folk Horror' - the lonely salt marshes of North Norfolk, the desolate sand dunes of coastal Suffolk, and the flat and isolated fens of Cambridgeshire.

Bordered by the unforgiving North Sea this region of strong and proud communities spanning several millennia - with its dark, foreboding, and liminal landscape - has spawned ancient traditions of folkloric myth and a history of pagan ritual all its own.

With the decline of the Gothic novel during the mid-19th century which heralded the arrival of the Ghost story with influential authors such as J. T. Sheridan Le Fanu, Edgar Allan Poe, Charlotte Riddell, Edith Wharton, and M. R. James taking centre stage, the scene was set for those modern era authors from whom I have taken much of my inspiration, with the works of Shirley Jackson, Susan Hill, James Herbert and Ramsey Campbell packing my bookshelves (apologies if I've omitted your favourite).

Both classic and modern ghost stories tend to contain elements of folklore and psychology - set within an isolated village or community, or within the walls of a knowing and unforgiving large house or structure of decaying magnificence.

Into this setting is placed the protagonist who is often of a quiet and naïve disposition, who then proceeds to discover some type of antiquarian object that introduces a spectral or paranormal threat into the mix.

Merge the two - fuse them, and this is what I term as :

'Folk Horror styled Ghost Stories - with elements of Mystery, Suspense and History'

Contents

Chapter One

First Warnings.

Captain Richard Headley, tall and broad-shouldered with angular features and thoughtful eyes, stepped out of the Austin Seven motorcar alongside Corporal Stan Meadows, his older and recently allotted driver, whose lively disposition was an antithesis to Richard's quiet demeanour. They had arrived in the remote seaside village of Hindringham Novers in Norfolk, their conversation punctuated by the occasional squawk of seagulls overhead.

"Never thought I'd come back here, sir," said Corporal Meadows, stretching out his limbs as he surveyed the once familiar surroundings. "It's been over thirty years since I've been to this old place."

"Your roots run deep, don't they, Corporal?" Richard replied, a hint of a smile on his lips as he took in the isolated village, its atmosphere untouched by time.

Hindringham Novers was a place suspended in 'Olde' England, as though the pages of history had somehow become entwined with the present day. Tidy cottages lined the narrow lanes, their white-washed walls adorned with climbing roses, while neatly trimmed hedgerows framed the landscape like an artist's masterpiece. The air was thick with the scent of salty sea breeze mixed with the earthy aroma of freshly turned soil from the nearby fields.

"Indeed, sir. I grew up not too far from here in Sheringham, but it feels like a lifetime ago," Corporal Meadows replied, his ordinarily jovial tone tinged with nostalgia.

As they walked toward the heart of the village, the small harbour came into view, its waters gently lapping at the pier's wooden planks. A handful of fishing boats laid at anchor close to shore, their sails furled, and nets piled haphazardly on the decks. Though modest in size, the harbour was as much a part of the community as the villagers themselves, the lifeblood of the local economy.

"Beautiful, isn't it?" Richard mused aloud, his gaze lingering on the quaint scene before them. "One can almost forget the world's troubles in a place like this."

"Perhaps so, sir," Corporal Meadows agreed, his eyes scanning the horizon as though searching for something more. "But even in paradise, there's always a serpent lurking."

Richard frowned at the cryptic remark but decided to let it pass, the enigmatic charm of Hindringham Novers already working under his skin. As they continued their exploration of the village, Richard couldn't shake the feeling that there was more to this idyllic place than met the eye.

"Come on," he said to Corporal Meadows – voice firm with purpose. "Let's find my lodgings for the night so that I can settle in. I have much to do tomorrow."

Richard stood at the edge of the harbour, watching the sun dip lower towards the horizon as it cast its light on the shimmering waters, his serenity tempered by the knowledge of his impending task - to find and secure potential defensive positions along the Norfolk and Suffolk coast. After the fall of Poland and the Germans positioning themselves to do the same to France and the Low Countries, Britain was facing an uncertain future. The urgency of fortifying the coast weighed heavily on his mind.

"Sir," Corporal Meadows said, approaching from behind. "I've secured your lodgings at The Black Shuck Inn. I'll be heading off now to visit my mother in Sheringham if there's nothing else you need."

"Very well, Corporal," Richard nodded, glancing at the quaint inn that would serve as his base of operations for the next few days. "We'll reconvene in three days to discuss our plans."

"Understood, sir." The Corporal saluted, got into the Austin Seven, and drove off, leaving Richard to make his way to The Black Shuck Inn alone.

As he entered the inn, the warmth and cosiness of the place enveloped him. The low ceilings and dark wooden beams spoke of a history that stretched back centuries. Richard could feel the weight of countless stories and secrets that had unfolded within these walls.

"Evening, sir," greeted the innkeeper, a stout man with a bushy moustache. "Welcome to The Black Shuck Inn. You must be Captain Headley."

"Indeed, I am," Richard replied, offering a polite smile. "I trust my corporal has made the necessary arrangements for my room?"

"Of course, Captain," the innkeeper confirmed, handing Richard a key. "You're in Room three, just up the stairs there. We've prepared a hearty meal for you as well. It should be ready in the dining area shortly."

"Thank you," Richard said gratefully, taking the key and climbing the creaky stairs to his room. He couldn't help but notice the curious glances from the other patrons, their whispers and furtive looks following him.

Once inside his room, Richard unpacked his belongings and laid out a map of the area on a small table. He studied it intently, marking potential locations for defensive positions with a pencil. The task was both exciting and daunting, as Richard knew that the security of the coastline depended on the strategic recommendations he would make to the Directorate of Fortifications and Works within the War Office, or FW3, as it was now known. It's vital that we stay ahead of any potential threat, he thought to himself.

The aroma of roasted meat wafted up from downstairs, reminding him of the meal awaiting him. He set aside his work for now and returned to the dining area, where the waitress set a plate piled high with food before him. Richard couldn't help but overhear snippets of conversation around him as he ate.

"Strange times we live in," one man muttered, shaking his head.

"Indeed," another agreed.

"But at least we have the Captain here to protect us," a rotund lady with ruddy cheeks and blue-grey hair nodded to Richard.

Richard nodded politely but could feel several sets of eyes on him as if waiting for a verbal response. Head down, he remained focused on his meal, determined to keep his thoughts private, even if the villagers were already spreading the word of his arrival.

The sun dipped lower in the sky with the shadows lengthening as Richard strolled through its narrow streets. The air was thick with the scent of wood smoke and salt, a heady mix that spoke of both the land's bounty and the sea's wrath. His studded shoes echoed against the cobblestones, drawing curious eyes from behind lace curtains.

An elderly woman greeted him as she swept her doorstep, "Evenin', Captain." Her voice held a note of hesitance as if unsure whether to trust this newcomer.

Richard tipped his cap respectfully, "Evening, ma'am," acknowledging her presence without breaking pace.

He could feel the villagers' wariness towards him, watching him from behind their cottage windows, sharing whispered conversations in hushed tones.

"Best be careful 'round these parts, Captain," called out a grizzled fisherman mending his nets by the harbour. "There be old ways here, and folks don't take kindly to strangers messin' with 'em."

Richard paused and turned to face the man, sensing the genuine concern in his words. "I appreciate the warning, sir. I have no intention of disturbing your traditions or customs. My only concern is the defence of our coastline."

"Ah, well," the fisherman said, scratching his beard. "Just mind ye don't go pokin' around where ye ain't wanted. There be things in this village best left alone." With that cryptic statement, the man returned to his work, leaving Richard to ponder his words as he walked away.

What secrets could this village hold? Richard wondered, feeling his curiosity piqued. I'm here for a specific purpose . . . but something about this place calls to me. It's as if the very stones hold whispers of the past. He shook off the thought, reminding himself of his duty. Defensive positions first, then I can satisfy my scholarly and archaeological interests.

As he continued his walk through Hindringham Novers, Richard couldn't help but notice the wary expressions that greeted him at every turn. The villagers were guarding something – their customs, beliefs, even their way of life. Though it was not his intention to disrupt their world, Richard knew that the importance of his task could not be understated. And so, he vowed to tread carefully, respecting their boundaries while fulfilling his duty.

Wandering the narrow, cobbled streets, Richard couldn't help but feel a growing sense of intrigue. The villagers' warnings echoed in his mind, stirring something deep within him – a desire to unearth the secrets that permeated the very air around him. He knew it was not his place to pry into their lives, but as a professional archaeologist, he could not resist the pull of the unknown.

"Curious," he whispered under his breath as he passed by neat rows of farming cottages, with each building telling its own tale of times gone by, with aged stone walls, thatched roofs, and ivy creeping up their facades. It was as though the village had been preserved in amber, untouched by the passing years.

"Good day to you, sir," called out a burly farmer, pitch-forking hay into a wheelbarrow. His eyes narrowed as they met Richard's, and he gave the Captain a curt nod. "You'd best watch your step around here. We don't take kindly to strangers meddling in our affairs."

"Of course," Richard replied, offering a tight-lipped smile. "I assure you, I have no intention of doing so – I'm here on official War Office duties, and I'll be gone once I've completed my work. I've no intention of causing any problems."

"See that you remember that." The farmer grumbled, turning back to his work without another word.

Richard continued his exploration, his gaze drawn to the small harbour that lay nestled between the sea and the low rock escarpments

- for what passed as cliffs in this flatter part of Britain. The fishing boats continued their rhythmic bobbing on the water. Weathered fishermen's cottages stood guard nearby, their sea-green shutters flapping in the breeze.

"Quite a sight, isn't it?" remarked an old fisherman, smoking a pipe as he leaned against the railing of a nearby cottage. He eyed Richard warily, as though weighing the worth of his words.

"Indeed it is," Richard agreed, noting the man's cautious demeanour. "I've never seen a village quite like this one. It feels . . . timeless."

"Timeless, eh?" The fisherman took a thoughtful puff of his pipe. "Aye, that's one word for it. But there are things hidden beneath the surface here, Captain. Things best left undisturbed."

"Is that so?" Richard asked, curiosity piqued. "I'm not here to uproot any secrets, just carrying out my duty."

"Very well then, best see you do that," the fisherman said, nodding slowly. "Just remember, some things should be left alone."

As Richard walked away, he couldn't shake the feeling that the villagers' warnings were more than mere superstition. There was something about Hindringham Novers that called to him, beckoning him to delve deeper into . . . what?

He was not sure. But for now, he was hungry and tired.

Chapter Two

Unseen Oaks.

D awn's first light seeped through the gap in the heavy curtains, casting a pale glow across Richard's face. He stirred and opened his eyes with a sigh, having spent a restless night tossing and turning in the unfamiliar bed. The villagers' odd behaviour the day before played on his mind; their suspicious glances and hushed conversations left him feeling uneasy.

"Damn them," he muttered under his breath as he swung his legs over the side of the mattress and sat up. His scientific rationale warred with the unsettling atmosphere that had pervaded his dreams, leaving him tense and bleary-eyed. He needed something to take his mind off of it all.

With a deep inhale, Richard pushed himself up from the bed and made his way to the washstand in the corner of the room. The cool water did little to ease the tension in his neck and shoulders, but at least it cleared some of the cobwebs from his mind. Richard's stomach grumbled loudly, surprising him as he had had a hearty meal the night before.

"Enough of this nonsense," he said firmly, donning his dressing gown and making his way down to the inn's dining room. "A good breakfast should set me straight."

"Morning, sir," the innkeeper greeted him with what Richard took for a somewhat forced smile. "What can I get you for breakfast?"

"Good morning," Richard replied, trying to sound as friendly as possible. "I'm rather famished, so I'll have the full works - bacon, eggs, tomato, mushrooms, and some buttered toast with marmalade, please. Oh, and a large pot of tea, if you would be so kind."

"Very well, sir," the innkeeper said, jotting down the order before disappearing into the kitchen.

As Richard waited, he took a moment to examine the other patrons in the dining room, trying to discern their thoughts and motives behind the cold reception he'd received. But their faces revealed nothing, leaving him with an uneasy feeling that only intensified his hunger.

"Here you are, sir," the innkeeper announced, returning with a steaming plate of food and a large pot of tea. "Enjoy your meal."

"Thank you," Richard said, his mouth already watering at the sight of the feast before him. He wasted no time tucking in, savouring each bite as if it were his last.

As he ate, his mind wandered back to the villagers and their peculiar behaviour. He tried to reason with himself that there must be a logical explanation for it all, but the nagging feeling in the pit of his stomach refused to abate.

With his hunger sated, Richard washed and dressed and left the inn to make his way towards the general store he had spotted on his arrival the day before. The morning air was crisp and invigorating, a welcome contrast to the stifling atmosphere of the inn.

Richard couldn't help but notice the villagers casting suspicious glances in his direction as he approached the store. Their unease was palpable, but he refused to let it affect him the way it had the day before. He pushed open the door, the bell above jingling merrily, a stark contradiction to the outside.

"Morning," Richard greeted the shopkeeper, who merely grunted in response. Undeterred, he perused the newspapers on display and selected a copy of The Times, though he usually preferred other publications. He paid for his purchase and exited the store, feeling the weight of the shopkeeper's gaze on his back.

Richard settled on a bench overlooking the picturesque village green and pond, hoping to lose himself in the world of newsprint and ink as he caught up on the events from across the Channel. But as he began to read, something in the corner of his eye caught his attention. A group of children had gathered nearby, engrossed in a game that seemed innocent at first glance. Yet, as he observed them more closely, Richard couldn't shake the feeling that there was something sinister about their play.

Unable to tear his eyes away from the unsettling performance, the children appeared to be enacting some form of ritual, complete with eerie chants and what looked like mock sacrifices. Though he knew little of pagan practices, Richard couldn't help but suspect that the game held darker implications than mere child's play.

Despite his growing unease, Richard forced himself to focus on the newspaper in his hands, refusing to give credence to the superstitious fears that seemed to grip the village. He shook his head, muttering under his breath, "I won't be swayed by such nonsense."

As he headed back to the inn, Richard's gaze was drawn to a grove of trees situated on a high point of land in the distance. It struck him as odd that he hadn't noticed them before; they seemed to stand sentinel over the village, their dark branches reaching skyward like gnarled fingers.

"Why didn't I see them yesterday?" he mused, the grove now firmly rooted in his thoughts. Something about its location and prominence piqued Richard's curiosity, but he decided to put it aside for now and return to the inn, where he could make further inquiries.

Back at the inn, Richard once more spread his maps across the table in his room, searching for any indication of the grove he had spotted earlier. The morning sun streamed through the window, casting long shadows on the yellowed pages as he traced his fingers over the intricate lines and symbols.

"Curious," he muttered, frustration mounting as he cross-referenced various maps yet found no mention of the grove. He leaned back in his chair, rubbing his temples. "Why isn't it marked? It's clearly visible from the village."

His mind, ever strategic, began to assess the potential value of the grove. From what he'd observed, it occupied a commanding position overlooking the village and the surrounding countryside. In military terms, it would make for an excellent observation post.

"Perhaps it has some significance to the villagers," Richard mused, considering their strange behaviour. "But that doesn't explain why it's absent from the maps."

He stood up abruptly and paced the room, his thoughts running wild. Was it a deliberate omission or simply an oversight? And what of the children's disturbing game? And the constant warnings for him to not meddle?

Richard couldn't help but feel a growing sense of unease as he pondered these questions. His rational mind struggled to reconcile the villagers' superstitions with his own scientific approach. Yet, despite his scepticism, he couldn't shake the nagging feeling that something was amiss.

"Enough," he declared, folding the maps and stacking them on the table. "I'll deal with this later. For now, I need a break."

With a deep breath, Richard pushed aside his concerns and headed downstairs, hoping that a mid-morning pot of tea would clear his head and provide him with some much-needed perspective on the perplexing situation at hand.

As the innkeeper placed the tray of tea and biscuits on the table, Richard decided to bring up the matter of the grove with him and a few locals who had gathered in the bar. He poured a cup of tea, then settled into an armchair near the fireplace, taking note of the framed maps adorning the walls around him. The room hummed with quiet conversation, the scent of pipe smoke thick in the air.

"Excuse me," he started, addressing the innkeeper as the man busied himself arranging logs by the fireplace. "I couldn't help but notice a grove of trees on the hill overlooking the village earlier today. Rather striking, isn't it?"

The innkeeper paused, glancing towards the group of locals who had abruptly fallen silent. "Aye, it's been there a long time," he replied cautiously.

"Strange thing is," Richard continued, stirring sugar into his tea. "I tried to locate it on the maps you have hanging in here and the ones I have upstairs, but it doesn't seem to appear on any of them. Is there a reason for that?"

The innkeeper hesitated, exchanging glances with the other men before replying, "Can't say for certain, sir. Perhaps it's just been overlooked."

"Overlooked?" Richard echoed, raising an eyebrow. The villagers shifted uncomfortably, their eyes darting away from his gaze. "It seems like quite a prominent feature - and one that could serve as an excellent observation post."

"Perhaps," the innkeeper conceded, now behind the bar counter and polishing a glass. "But it's not something we concern ourselves with here."

"Forgive my curiosity," Richard said, sipping his tea. "It's just that I've never encountered such a discrepancy between what I see and what has been recorded."

"Sometimes things are best left unrecorded," a grizzled local chimed in, puffing on his pipe. "We don't meddle in what's beyond our understanding."

"Beyond your understanding?" Richard asked, his curiosity piqued. He sensed the villagers were holding something back and found himself eager to uncover the truth behind their reticence.

"Old legends and superstitions," another man muttered, scratching his beard. "Nothing worth bothering your head about."

"Still," Richard insisted, "I can't help but wonder if there's more to the grove than meets the eye. Surely you must have some inkling as to its significance?"

The locals once more exchanged uneasy glances, and the innkeeper sighed. "It's true that there are stories, Captain Headley. There are dark tales of long-forgotten rituals and strange happenings up there on the hill. But they're just that – stories. Best not to give them any currency."

"Perhaps," Richard conceded, swallowing a mouthful of tea. His scientific mind warred with the ghostly whispers that seemed to cling to the villagers' words. Yet, despite his doubts, he couldn't deny the allure of the unknown. Now shrouded in mystique, the grove called to him like a siren song.

Richard leaned back in his chair, taking in the solemn expressions on the faces of those around him. They truly believed in the tales they shared, and the weight of their words hung heavily in the air.

"Thank you for indulging my curiosity," he said, pushing aside his empty teacup. "I'll leave you to your conversations."

Richard's thoughts churned as he retreated to the sanctuary of his room, intertwining the rational and the inexplicable. Once a mere curiosity, the grove had become an enigma that begged to be solved, and he found himself unable to resist its pull.

The light wind rustled the leaves of the trees outside the inn, casting dappled shadows on the worn cobblestones below. Richard stood by the window, watching villagers go about their daily routines, their whispered conversations punctuated by furtive glances in the direction of his room. The grove still loomed over him, both figuratively and literally, as he grappled with the notion of defying the locals' advice.

"Superstition," he muttered, shaking his head. "Surely there's a rational explanation for their reticence."

His fingers drummed against the windowsill, his thoughts straying to the children he'd seen earlier playing that strange game. A vague sense of unease washed over him as if the very atmosphere of the village was seeping into his bones.

"Ridiculous," he scoffed, turning away from the window. "I'm allowing these people's nonsensical beliefs to cloud my judgment."

He paced the room, trying to reconcile his scientific mindset with the supernatural fears held by the villagers. It was as if two opposing forces were at war within him: the methodical, analytical part of his mind that sought empirical explanations and an inexplicable fascination with the unknown that threatened to pull him deeper into the shadows.

"Perhaps I should investigate the grove myself," he mused aloud. "Uncover the truth behind these stories and put an end to this foolishness."

"Best be careful, sir," a voice called from the doorway. Richard turned to see the innkeeper standing there, his brow furrowed with concern. "The door was ajar, sir, and I heard you talking to yourself as I passed," he took a step into the room and, lowering his voice, said, "Folks 'round here don't take kindly to strangers pokin' their noses where they don't belong."

"Thank you for your warning," Richard replied, his tone curter than he intended. "But I am not one to blindly accept superstition without seeking a reasonable explanation."

"Suit yourself, sir," the innkeeper said with a shrug. "Just remember – some things are best left undisturbed."

With that, he retreated down the hallway, leaving Richard to wrestle with his decision alone.

"Undisturbed!" Richard echoed, his gaze drifting back to the window and the distant grove. An unexpected wave of fatigue washed over him, the weight of his broken sleep and inner turmoil suddenly bearing down on him.

"Perhaps I should rest first," he conceded, feeling his eyes grow heavy. "There will be time enough to explore the grove later."

He crossed the room to his bed, the creaking floorboards protesting beneath his boots. As he lay down, his thoughts still swirled around the mysterious grove and the villagers' inexplicable fears, and as he closed his eyes, the shadows seemed to recede, at least for a while, as he surrendered to the welcoming embrace of sleep.

A sudden cacophony of crows cawing outside his window jolted Richard awake. He sat up, disoriented for a moment before the memory of the grove and the villagers' strange behaviour flooded back into his consciousness. Glancing at the clock on the bedside table, he noticed that only an hour or so had passed since he'd lain down to rest.

"Time enough for lunch," he mused, rubbing the sleep from his eyes. With renewed determination, he rose from the bed and smoothed out the wrinkles in his clothes. The mystery of the grove still tugged at him like a loose thread, and he couldn't help but feel that unravelling it might hold the key to understanding this peculiar village.

Descending the creaky staircase, the aroma of freshly baked bread and vegetable soup wafted towards him, stirring his appetite. As he entered the dining room, he spotted the innkeeper behind the counter, wiping down the back bar shelving with a rag.

"Ah, Captain Headley, I trust you had a good rest?" the innkeeper asked with genuine warmth in his voice despite their earlier disagreement.

"Indeed, thank you," Richard replied, taking a seat at a small corner table. "I must admit, your beds are quite comfortable."

"Nothing but the best for our guests," the innkeeper said with a smile, approaching Richard's table. "Would you care for some soup and bread? It's a local speciality, made fresh every day."

"Sounds delightful," Richard agreed, his stomach rumbling in anticipation. "And perhaps another pot of tea if it's not too much trouble."

"Of course, sir," the innkeeper said, already turning to prepare the order. "I'll have it all brought to you shortly."

Richard let his gaze wander around the dimly lit dining room as he waited. A few locals were scattered about, nursing their drinks and murmuring in hushed tones. He couldn't help but wonder if they were discussing him and his interest in the grove.

"Am I really so threatening?" he thought, frowning slightly. "I'm merely trying to understand this place and its mysteries."

Before long, the innkeeper returned with a steaming bowl of soup, a basket of warm bread, and a fresh pot of tea. Richard thanked him and tucked into his meal, savouring the hearty flavours that seemed to embody the essence of the countryside.

As he ate, he couldn't help but overhear snippets of conversation from the neighbouring tables – discussions of crop yields, livestock births, and other mundane aspects of farming and village life. Yet beneath it all, he sensed an undercurrent of unease, a shared sense of wariness that seemed to pervade the very air.

"Is it me or the grove?" he wondered, sipping his tea. "Or perhaps, in their superstitious minds, the villagers are inextricably linking the two."

He paused, a sudden realization dawning on him. Could his presence here be somehow intertwined with the mystery of the grove?

"Ridiculous," he chided himself, shaking his head. "I'm letting their superstitions get the better of me."

With a resolute sigh, Richard finished his lunch and pushed the empty bowl away. Whatever the villagers might think of him, he knew that he was no ghost or harbinger of doom. He was simply a curious man with a thirst for knowledge – and the mystery surrounding the grove was making him more curious as time went on.

Chapter Three

Chalk Marks and Symbols.

The aroma of freshly baked bread and meaty soup lingered in the air.

Richard couldn't help but notice the sideways glances and hushed whispers of the villagers around him, their words obscured by the clink of cutlery and the crackling fire. Richard was well aware that he had become a subject of interest, viewed as an outsider who had arrived to pry into their lives and secrets.

He knew he couldn't afford to be distracted by idle gossip or superstition; there was work to be done, and he needed to focus on that. Rising from the table, Richard returned to his room and collected his belongings: a sturdy leather bag, his trusty notebook filled with meticulous notes, and a measuring tape that had served him well over the years.

Richard stepped out into the bright early afternoon sun, determined to make some progress. His boots crunched against the gravel pathway, as he strode off towards the grove that he was now sure had been the topic of so many whispered conversations. Despite his resolve, he couldn't shake the nagging unease that had taken root deep within him.

Richard mulled over the information he had gathered about the grove as he strolled, the sun warming his face. Why was the grove absent from the maps? What could possibly be so terrifying about a simple stand of trees? He tried to dismiss the strange attitudes of the villagers and their baseless warnings, reminding himself that he was a man of science and logic, not one to be swayed by primitive fears.

"Superstitions and legends have no place in my work," he thought, pushing onwards. "I will find the truth behind this grove, whilst I remain objective and rational."

The village fading behind him as he crossed the picturesque countryside, Richard's eyes scanned the horizon, taking in the gentle slope of the ancient landscape that stretched out before him; a landscape that seemed to be at odds with the tales the villagers had woven around the grove, and he couldn't help but marvel at the beauty of his surroundings.

"Perhaps these villagers have allowed their fears to overshadow the simple splendour of nature," Richard mused, his mind already constructing an argument to counter any irrational claims he might encounter.

With each step, he grew more confident in his convictions, "It's just a grove of trees, after all."

As the sun cast its golden rays across the land, Richard was certain he was on the right path, both literally and metaphorically. With all its mystery and intrigue, the grove awaited him up ahead - a challenge that he would meet head-on, armed with reason and unwavering determination.

An eerie silence enveloped Richard as he stepped into the grove, the very atmosphere thick with a palpable stillness. The sunlight filtering through the ancient trees cast dappled shadows upon the mossy ground, further intensifying the sense of otherworldliness that seemed to pervade this place.

It was as if the grove existed outside of time, a sanctuary untouched by the modern world.

"Focus on the task at hand," Richard reminded himself, his voice barely above a whisper; yet disturbing him by how it broke the unnatural quiet. He shook off the unsettling feeling and reached for the notebook in his bag, trying not to let the whispers of superstition from the villagers cloud his judgment. "This grove may hold the key to their strange behaviour, but I must approach it clearly, rationally."

He consulted his notes, checking the specific area he had identified as a potential defensive site. His fingers traced the treeless map's contour lines, eyes narrowing as he compared the map with the terrain before him. This location offered a strategic vantage point, with a clear view of the coastline and the village below. It was a perfect position.

"Could the legends surrounding this place really be nothing more than folklore?" Richard wondered, his curiosity gnawing at him despite his determination to remain objective. "Or is something darker lurking beneath the surface, something they are afraid to confront?"

"Preposterous," he muttered, scolding himself for entertaining such thoughts. He was a man of science and reason, not one to be swayed by baseless rural fears.

Richard paced the area, measuring tape in hand, as he methodically calculated distances between the trees and the angle of potential sightlines. The grove's eerie stillness remained, but he pushed it to the back of his mind, focusing on the task at hand. As he moved among the ancient trees, he couldn't help but feel a sense of awe at their sheer size and age; these silent giants had borne witness to countless generations of humanity, yet, they stood unmoved by the passages of time.

"Twelve yards from this oak to the next," he murmured, making notes in his weathered notebook, "and another nine yards between the other two." Despite the overwhelming silence, Richard found solace in giving voice to his thoughts, as though by doing so, he could assert his rationality over the superstitions that seemed to shroud the grove.

As he continued to assess the area, his keen and analytical mind recalled the briefings and instruction he had received in Cambridge, on how to evaluate defensive positions and the suitability of terrain for constructing the newly designed pill boxes.

When he had agreed to be seconded from his position as a senior surveyor with the Ancient Monuments Branch within the Office of Woods, Forests, Land Revenues, Works, and Buildings, to take up a position with the Directorate of Fortifications and Works within the War Office, he had been pleasantly surprised that the posting came with a slight bump-up on his already reasonable salary.

Not that money was a contributing factor as, like many, he had readily accepted the call to King and Country, with the outbreak of another war with Germany only six weeks earlier. His experience serving in the Cambridge University Officers Training Corps, when he was reading Archaeology at Kings College nearly two decades before, now standing him in good stead. The rank of Captain, albeit non-combatant, was commensurate with his service record and professional standing.

Pausing in his note taking, he was confident that defenders could monitor the coast road from this position and easily spot any approaching threats. Furthermore, the natural barrier of the sandstone cliffs only a mile to the north would limit enemy movements, giving the defenders a clear advantage. Yes, this grove held significant potential as a defensive stronghold.

Satisfied with his assessment, he took a piece of chalk and began marking the ancient trees that would have to be felled to make way for the pill box.

Richard marked another tree as the sun dipped lower in the sky, casting long, gnarled shadows through the grove. He worked quickly and efficiently, the white chalk lines stood out sharply against the ancient bark, each stroke a deliberate decision.

"Sometimes," he mused quietly, "the greatest threat isn't posed by an external force, but in our own inability to adapt and change."

As he marked the final tree, Richard couldn't help but feel a sense of accomplishment – he had undertaken his first evaluation of a prospective defensive site, emerging with a rational plan to protect the wider area and the village of Hindringham Novers in particular. The grove's mysteries remained, but they were no longer his primary concern.

"Let the villagers hold onto their superstitions," he thought as he pocketed the chalk and surveyed his handiwork. "I have done my duty and will stand by it, come what may." With that resolution firmly in place, Richard gathered his belongings and prepared to leave the grove behind, its secrets still shrouded in shadows, yet no longer able to cast doubt upon his mission.

Stooping down to pick up his bag, Richard paused as he noticed several distinct lines in the moss clinging to an area of exposed roots.

Kneeling, he examined the markings more closely: peculiar symbols – fresh and distinct, the edges still sharp, with the chisel or knife marks evident.

"Strange," he muttered to himself, running his fingers over the intricate lines. He couldn't recall ever seeing such symbols in his studies or travels. His mind raced with possible explanations – perhaps local folklore or the work of idle hands and pranksters seeking to maintain the village's mysterious reputation.

Richard strode over to the closest tree. Similar marks on the roots of this as on the other. Then checking several other trees, he found the same result. Why had he not noticed them before?

An unsettling sense of unease washed over him, momentarily causing his rational thoughts to falter. He shook his head, dismissing any supernatural notions that tried to creep into his mind. "No," he said firmly under his breath, "there's a reasonable explanation for all this."

As the shadows in the grove lengthened, they seemed to take on lives of their own, twisting and contorting into unnatural shapes that danced at the edge of Richard's vision. The air grew colder, as if a sudden frost had descended upon the area, sending shivers down his spine. He rubbed his hands together, trying to ward off the chill that seeped into his bones.

"Damn this weather," he muttered under his breath not wanting to be affected by the eerie atmosphere that now enveloped him. His practical mind clung to rational explanations, attributing the strange sensations to the natural elements rather than any supernatural influence.

With grim determination, Richard gave one last look around the grove and turned to leave; as he did, the sensation of being watched swept over him, as though unseen eyes bore into him from every direction.

"Mustn't let imagination get the better of me," he thought, resisting the urge to glance over his shoulder.

Despite his efforts to maintain a sense of order, Richard couldn't shake off the nagging feeling that he had trespassed on forbidden ground. Every creak of the branches above, every rustle of leaves beneath his feet, seemed to echo with a disapproving murmur, urging him to leave the grove and never return.

As Richard shouldered his bag and turned to make his way back towards the village, the oppressive stillness of the grove seemed to close in around him, as if reluctant to let him leave its shadowy grasp.

"Keep moving," he urged himself, quickening his pace. "It's just the wind and the shadows playing tricks." His heart raced in his chest, a small voice whispering in the recess of his mind that perhaps there was more to the village's secrets and mysteries than mere superstition.

Swallowing the lump of fear that had lodged in his throat Richard stepped out of the grove and back into the sunlight, leaving behind the twisted shadows and eerie chill. As he strode purposefully away, he felt the lingering sensation of unseen eyes watching him from the depths of the grove, promising to haunt his thoughts for days to come.

At the foot of the slope leading from the grove, Richard joined the narrow country lane leading back to the village, his boots crunching against the gravel with each step. The grove's ominous presence still lingered in his mind like an unwelcome guest, and now with some distance between him and the mighty oaks, he couldn't help but glance over his shoulder at regular intervals. The weight of unseen eyes seemed to bore into his back, causing an involuntary shudder to race up his spine.

"Pull yourself together, man," he muttered under his breath. "It's just a grove of oaks, nothing more."

Yet, despite his best efforts, the sensation refused to abate. It clung to him like a cold, clammy mist that refused to dissipate under the bright sunlight. As he continued on, Richard found it increasingly difficult to ignore the stark contrast between the eerie grove and the idyllic countryside surrounding him.

The landscape appeared normal enough; recently harvested fields stretched out before him, their clean edged and dark furrows meeting on the horizon. Birds flitted through the air, their melodies providing a soothing soundtrack to his journey. Even the sun seemed to shine brighter than before, casting a warm glow over the Norfolk countryside.

"Everything is as it should be," he thought, grasping for any shred of rationality to banish the lingering dread. "There's no reason for this unease."

But Richard's attempts at self-assurance were futile, for the disquiet remained like a stubborn stain on his thoughts. He found himself questioning every rustle in the bushes, every tree branch creak, as if expecting some malevolent force to reveal itself.

"Stop it," he chided himself, giving a frustrated shake of his head. "You're letting your imagination run wild. These people have filled your head with nonsense, that's all."

He tried to focus on the task at hand, replaying the measurements he'd taken and mentally preparing the report he would write up later in his room at the inn. But even as he delved into the familiar mental territory of organised and methodical procedure, the feeling in his mind that something was amiss refused to be silenced.

"Maybe it's just their way of protecting their traditions," he mused, attempting to rationalise the villagers' guarded behaviour. "Perhaps they've created these stories as a means of preserving their way of life. To keep strangers at bay."

But even as Richard attempted to weave a logical explanation for his unease, the haunting sensation of being watched persisted, doggedly clawing at the edges of his consciousness. He couldn't escape the nagging feeling that there was more to the village's secrets than mere superstition and folklore. And though he tried to dismiss it as a product of his overactive imagination, the unshakable chill that had settled in his bones told him otherwise.

"Enough!" he exclaimed, drawing a deep breath, and forcing himself to focus on the road ahead. "I have a job to do, and I won't let these fanciful notions distract me."

With renewed determination, Richard strode onward, every step taking him further from the grove and its mysteries. But as he made his way back towards the village, the lingering sense of unease continued to gnaw at him, like an itch he couldn't quite reach; haunted by the unseen eyes that seemed to watch his every move.

Approaching the village, Richard noticed the locals going about their day, seemingly unaffected by the ominous presence of the grove that loomed over them. Their seemingly easy conversations only served to heighten his growing paranoia, making him feel all the more isolated in his mounting fear.

"Good afternoon, sir," the grocer who had sold him the newspaper greeted him, as he swept the pavement area outside his shop. His smile seemed forced and did nothing to alleviate Richard's unease.

"Afternoon," Richard replied, forcing a tight-lipped smile before continuing on his way. If anything, the normalcy of the scene grated against his heightened nerves, making it even more difficult for him to shake off the lingering dread.

When he finally reached the inn, Richard paused at the threshold, his hand resting on the worn brass handle of the door. The warm glow of the hearth beckoned him inside, but the weight of the grove's presence still clung to him like a cold fog. He drew a deep breath, trying to will away the unsettling sensation that was starting to become all too familiar in the village.

"Get a grip, Richard," he admonished himself. "It's just an old grove and some silly symbols. Nothing more."

But even as he stepped into the cozy interior of the inn, the dread that had followed him from the grove refused to dissipate. It seemed to seep into the very walls of the building, casting long shadows that twisted and contorted with every flicker of the firelight.

"Captain Headley, back already?" greeted the innkeeper, looking up from pulling a pint at the bar. "Did you find what you were looking for?"

"More or less," Richard replied noncommittally, his thoughts consumed by the grove and the symbols he had discovered there. He knew that he couldn't share his findings with the villagers without stirring up their superstitions and potentially inciting yet more antagonism against him.

"Very well, sir. Dinner will be in one hour," the innkeeper nodded as Richard made his way up the stairs to his room. As he climbed, the sense of unease only intensified with each creaking step, leaving him feeling like some unseen force was pursuing him.

Once inside the sanctuary of his room, Richard sank into a chair, his eyes scanning the maps strewn across the desk before him. "Damn it all," he whispered, gripping his hair in frustration. "What am I becoming?"

He knew he needed to focus on his task – his duty – but the secrets of the grove called out to him, like a siren song, threatening to pull him under and consume him entirely.

Chapter Four

Weight of Solitude.

The air hung heavy with the aroma from the kitchens as Richard picked at his dinner, the unsettling events of the day gnawing at him. The thick stew before him had once seemed appetizing, but now it lay cold and untouched. He took a mouthful from his pint of locally brewed ale, trying to quench the dryness that clung to the back of his throat.

His gaze flitted around The Black Shuck Inn, taking note of the curious villagers who eyed him with a mix of suspicion and whispered conversation. Their eyes darted away when they realized he was watching, but the hushed discussions continued, making him feel like a specimen under a microscope.

"Doesn't seem to be much of an appetite on you tonight, sir," the innkeeper remarked, approaching Richard's table. His voice held a hint of concern, but Richard couldn't help but think there was also an undertone of suspicion. "It's a shame to waste good food."

"Apologies," Richard replied, forcing a tight-lipped smile. "I suppose I'm just not as hungry as I thought." He mentally chastised himself for letting the village's eerie atmosphere affect him so deeply.

"Fair enough," the innkeeper said, eying Richard's uneaten meal before turning to attend to other patrons. As he walked away, Richard caught a glimpse of the innkeeper exchanging words with a burly man in the corner, their eyes flickering towards him briefly.

Richard watched as the evening wore on, groups of friends sharing stories and drinking together while he remained on the periphery. He couldn't shake the feeling that these people held secrets, which they guarded fiercely - entwined with the grove and its strange symbols.

"Something on your mind?" an old woman asked as she shuffled past, her voice as brittle as dried leaves. Richard looked up, startled by the intrusion.

"I... I beg your pardon?" Richard stammered, unprepared for the sudden interaction.

"Nothing good ever comes from poking your nose where it doesn't belong," she replied cryptically before shuffling on her way.

Richard stared after her, feeling the weight of her words settle heavily on his shoulders. He knew he should heed her warning and the warnings of others in the village, but his innate curiosity refused to be silenced.

The clatter of cutlery and the low murmur of conversation in The Black Shuck Inn did nothing to quell Richard's growing unease. His appetite had long since waned, replaced by a gnawing curiosity that burrowed deep within him.

"Looks like we've got some rain coming tonight," one villager remarked to another as he peered out the window. Richard strained to listen for any further information they might exchange but could only hear whispers and received furtive glances in his direction. The air seemed to hum with secrets, each tantalizingly out of reach.

"Are you sure everything's alright, Captain?" the innkeeper asked from behind the bar, his eyes narrowing with what Richard now took for thinly disguised suspicion. Richard forced a smile, attempting to mask his growing paranoia.

"Quite sure," he replied tersely, pushing away from the table. "I think I'll retire for the evening." He could feel the villagers' gazes following him as he ascended the stairs to his room. With each step, he wondered if their whispered words held any answers - did they know something about the grove and its unsettling symbols that they refused to share with outsiders?

The door to his room clicked shut behind him, separating him from the hushed voices and penetrating stares. Richard leaned back against the wooden frame, catching his breath and steadying his racing thoughts.

Richard moved about his small room, the floorboards creaking underfoot as he prepared for bed. He double-checked that the door was locked, and the window fastened before drawing the curtains and shutting out the night and any prying eyes. Despite his best efforts to remain rational, the unsettling events of the day had shaken him more than he cared to admit.

Richard's thoughts churned like the restless sea beyond the village as he lay in the unfamiliar bed. With its disturbing symbols and the villagers' whispered warnings, the grove played on a loop in his mind, each repetition increasing his unease.

Trying to quell his growing obsession with the grove, he muttered to himself, "There's nothing supernatural here, just superstition and secrets."

The darkness in the small room seemed to close in around him, suffocating and oppressive. His breathing grew shallow as he struggled to find sleep, his body tense with anticipation. In the dead of night, he startled awake to what he took as the sound of hushed voices from the corridor outside his room.

"Who's there?" he demanded, voice shaky with a mixture of fear and annoyance, his fingers gripping the bedsheets tightly. No response came, only the distant whispers of the wind outside mocking his paranoia.

Richard sat up, berating himself for allowing the villagers' tales to affect him so profoundly. "This is ridiculous," he thought, rubbing the sleep from his eyes. "I'm a man of science, not some damn superstitious fool. There's a logical explanation for everything."

But even as he tried to convince himself of this, a feeling of coldness gripped his heart, the icy tendrils of doubt creeping into every corner of his mind. He knew he could no longer ignore the strange occurrences surrounding the grove, nor could he shake the feeling that the villagers were hiding something sinister beneath their seemingly idyllic facade.

"Tomorrow," he promised himself, "I will find answers. I will uncover the truth behind this village and its secrets." Lighting a candle, purely for comfort, Richard placed it on the washstand in the corner and then settled back into his bed, his resolve hardened, driven by a desire to dispel his growing fears and prove that reason would triumph over superstition.

Slowly, his eyes grew heavy, weighed down with exhaustion and the day's events. The room filled with an eerie silence as Richard tried to calm his racing thoughts.

"Tomorrow," he whispered again in his half-sleep, his voice barely audible. "Tomorrow."

Eventually, sleep claimed him, offering a temporary reprieve from the shadows that threatened to consume him.

The candle's flickering flame cast eerie, elongated shadows on the walls of Richard's small room as he held his breath, listening intently for any sign of the hushed voices that had startled him awake. His heart raced in his chest, a frantic drumbeat. He couldn't shake the feeling that he was not alone, that something or someone lurked just beyond the edge of his vision, in the shadows that the candle could now not penetrate.

"Hello?" his voice barely more than a whisper as it wavered with uncertainty. "Is anyone there?"

There was no reply, save for the soft echo of his words bouncing off the walls, only adding to the unsettling atmosphere. Taking a deep breath, Richard steeled himself, swung his legs off the bed and crept towards the candle, whose flickering light barely pierced the oppressive darkness.

As he examined every shadowy corner of the room, his thoughts churned relentlessly, memories of the villagers' whispered conversations and enigmatic warnings swirling around his mind like a dark maelstrom. "Have I brought this upon myself with my curiosity?" he thought, trying to maintain his rational perspective despite the mounting fear threatening to consume him entirely.

"Ridiculous," he muttered under his breath, shaking his head to dispel the irrational thoughts. "There's nothing here but my imagination."

Finally, after what felt like an eternity, Richard completed his search, finding no signs of intrusion or hidden presence. The room was as empty and quiet as it had been when he'd first settled to sleep, offering no explanation for the voices disturbing his rest.

Exhausted and still trembling from the adrenaline coursing through his veins, Richard sank onto the edge of his bed, holding his pounding head in his cupped hands. He tried to slow his racing thoughts, focusing on his chest's steady rise and fall as he took deep, calming breaths.

"Get a grip, man," he whispered to himself, his voice strained. "You're letting superstition get the better of you. Tomorrow, you'll find rational explanations for all of this."

Yet, as he sat in the flickering candlelight, the creeping shadows and inexplicable voices still lingering in his mind, the certainty that had once fortified his resolve seemed to waver. He couldn't help but wonder whether the villagers' warnings and strange behaviour were not mere superstition but rather a genuine concern for something far more sinister than he could have imagined.

But for now, Richard knew he needed rest. Clinging to the hope that tomorrow would bring clarity and reason, he blew out the candle and lay back down on the bed, the darkness enveloping him like a shroud as he closed his eyes, trying to silence the disquieting thoughts that plagued his weary mind.

The relentless ticking of the old clock on the wall seemed to echo through the small room, serving as a cruel reminder of Richard's sleepless hours. He had been tossing and turning in bed, his body aching from the persistent tension that gripped him. His thoughts raced around the mysterious grove and the villagers' cryptic warnings, refusing to release their grip on his weary mind.

"Damn this place," Richard muttered under his breath, frustrated with how the day's events had left him feeling so vulnerable and exposed. He was a man of reason, not one to be swayed by the whispers of rural superstition. And yet, he couldn't deny the growing paranoia gnawing at him, like a worm burrowing deeper into the core of an apple.

As Richard lay there, sweat dampening his pillow, he tried to focus his thoughts on the task at hand: identifying defensive positions along the coast. The grove atop the hill had seemed promising, but now its haunting aura and those strange symbols carved into the roots threatened to overshadow everything else. He needed to regain control over his racing mind, to remind himself that logic and reason would triumph over any irrational fear.

"Those people don't know what they're talking about," Richard whispered to himself, trying to dismiss the villagers' anxiety as nothing more than baseless superstition. "It's just a grove of trees, for heaven's sake. There has to be a rational explanation for all this."

As Richard wrestled with his thoughts, he imagined himself back at Kings College, surrounded by books and scholarly companions who shared his dedication to pursuing knowledge. They would scoff at the notion of a cursed grove or dark rituals hidden in the heart of a sleepy village, and Richard tried to draw strength from their imagined scepticism. Yet, even as he sought solace in memories of his academic past, the cold fingers of doubt continued to tighten their grip on him.

"Maybe . . . maybe I'm just not as strong as I thought," Richard admitted, his voice barely audible; the admission weighed heavily on him.

"Enough!" he growled, clenching his fists and forcing himself to sit in bed. "I will not let this place get the better of me. Tomorrow, I will put these ridiculous thoughts behind me."

Richard tried to convince himself of the truth in his words as he spoke, but deep down, a nagging doubt still lingered. He knew that no matter how hard he tried to cling to reason, the combination of the village's eerie atmosphere and the villagers' growing paranoia threatened to consume him if he didn't find a way to dispel it.

But for now, all he could do was try to sleep and hope that the morning would bring a new perspective and a way out of the darkness that threatened to engulf him.

Chapter Five

Beyond the Silence.

Having finished breakfast, Richard decided it was time to delve deeper into the local history, so he headed to The Black Shuck Inn's private library. Passing the innkeeper's quarters, Richard pushed a note under the door requesting that he have lunch in his room.

Finding the library at the end of the corridor behind the bar, Richard stepped into the small room, immediately greeted by the musty scent of old leather, paper, and wood polish mingling in the air.

Richard was pleasantly surprised to find the small library so well stocked, particularly for such a remote village inn.

The room was dimly lit, sunlight filtering through the single salt-stained window, casting long shadows across the floor. Dust motes floated lazily in the air, disturbed by Richard's entrance, causing him to open one of the leaded lights to mitigate the now mildly fetid air.

Worn wooden shelves lined the walls with ancient tomes and manuscripts that seemed to whisper their secrets to anyone who might care to listen. The atmosphere was thick with the weight of centuries, like stepping back in time to a forgotten world.

Richard crossed over to the wall with floor-to-ceiling shelves, his fingers lightly brushing the spines of the books as he passed them. He had always known that it was his nature to be systematic in his approach, seeking out information efficiently and logically. As an archaeologist, he was accustomed to sifting through layers of history, piecing together fragments to form a coherent narrative. With its hidden treasures, this library presented a tantalizing challenge and opportunity.

As he searched for any volumes that might shed light on Hindringham Novers, the surrounding area – particularly the grove and its mysterious past - he couldn't help but feel a mounting excitement. The villagers' silence only fuelled his determination to uncover the truth. But he knew he had to be patient and methodical in his research. He recalled his days at King's College, where he had honed his skills in deciphering the complex histories behind artefacts and archaeological sites.

Settling into a worn armchair near the window, the leather creaking under his weight, he selected one of the half-dozen promising-looking titles he had taken from the shelves. The pages were yellowed and fragile, their edges threatening to crumble at the slightest touch. They contained accounts of local folklore, superstitions, and strange occurrences that seemed to be rooted in the very soil of this remote corner of North Norfolk. As Richard read, his excitement grew, his imagination running wild with possibilities. He could feel the hairs on the back of his neck stand on end as he became more and more consumed by the dark history hidden within the pages.

"Knowledge is the key," he whispered, echoing the words his father had drilled into him throughout his youth. And now, surrounded by these venerable texts, Richard felt closer than ever to unlocking the secrets he believed had been buried beneath the village's idyllic façade for so long.

Standing and stretching, Richard crossed the room to the shelves, the dust swirling in the dim light as his eyes scanned the book spines for any title that might convey more information about the village and its environs.

He nearly missed the small book, wedged, as it was, between two more prominent and ornate tomes, being small and relatively unassuming in appearance. With a cautious hand, he extracted it, and reseating himself in the leather chair, he carefully opened the first page. The fragile parchment crackled under his touch; the scent of decay and age filled his nostrils, starkly contrasting with the salty sea air of Hindringham Novers wafting through the open window. As he flipped through the pages, scanning the remarkably still clear and crisp text, Richard found himself drawn into the disturbing accounts of the village and the grove inscribed within.

"Missing villagers . . . suicide pacts . . . rumours of ritual sacrifices . . ." he muttered under his breath, his voice barely more than a whisper in the library's silence. The words seemed to echo in the confined space, weighing heavily on his chest.

Richard's curiosity and obsession grew stronger with each new revelation, becoming a gnawing hunger that refused to be sated. It was as if the darkness beneath the village's idyllic surface beckoned him, urging him to delve deeper into its hidden secrets.

He continued reading, his heart pounding in anticipation as his determination swelled. The eerie tales of the grove and its mysterious past consumed him, making it impossible to focus on anything else. The villagers' whispers and cryptic warnings over recent days only serving to fuel his desire for answers.

"Answers," he whispered, swallowing hard as he focussed intently on the book, his fingers trembling slightly. "I need to find answers."

Dust motes danced in the weak sunlight as Richard uncovered yet more disturbing accounts, drawing him deeper into the dark history of Hindringham Novers: more missing villagers, more unexplained deaths, more suicide pacts, and more sacrifices. With every new revelation, his curiosity grew.

"Curious," Richard mused, his voice barely above a whisper. He paused as he flicked through the book's end pages and traced the faint lines of an illustration depicting a grove of oaks, its dark silhouette looming ominously over the village. "So many lost souls, so much pain."

"Could it be?" he pondered, his brow furrowing as he tried to make connections between the various stories. "Is this the key that unlocks the mystery of the grove?"

Richard took meticulous notes, his penmanship neat and precise despite his eager haste. He sketched maps and diagrams, comparing them to the notes he had already made since his arrival in Hindringham Novers. Slowly but surely, a coherent narrative emerged from the tangled web of local lore.

"By God," he breathed, his eyes widening with realization. "There's something here... it's starting to make sense now."

His mind raced with possibilities and theories, each more unnerving than the last. He knew he was venturing onto treacherous ground, but the pursuit of truth had always been his guiding star, no matter how dark and twisted the path.

As Richard prepared to leave the library, he glanced once more at the illustration of the grove – was it the grove above this village? He couldn't be sure – yet its branches, like skeletal fingers, clawed at the sky. A shiver ran down his spine, but he refused to let fear deter him.

"Let the villagers whisper and scowl," he thought determinedly. "I will uncover their secrets and, in doing so, perhaps bring some measure of peace – if not to this troubled place – then to me."

Richard entered the dining room, the aroma of stewing tea wafting through the air. The mid-morning light streamed in through the windows, casting a warm glow across the room where several villagers sat, enjoying their own pots. He poured himself a cup and sat near them, determined to gather more information about the grove.

"Good morning," Richard greeted the group with a polite nod, his voice steady and measured. "I couldn't help but overhear some of your conversations yesterday when discussing farming and agricultural matters. I'm interested in the local history and folklore. Would any of you be willing to share your knowledge?"

The villagers exchanged wary glances, their expressions guarded as they shifted uneasily in their seats. One man, an older fellow with a weathered face, fixed Richard with a steely gaze.

"Best not to go poking around in things that don't concern you, Captain," he muttered gruffly, stirring his tea. "There's a reason we don't like talking about the past."

"Forgive me," Richard replied, undeterred. "I have no intention of causing trouble or disrespecting your customs. However, I believe that understanding the history of this place may help me in my current assignment."

"Leave well enough alone, sir," another villager chimed in, her voice firm but not unkind. "We've got our reasons for keeping quiet, and it's best you do respect that."

"Please," Richard implored, his frustration simmering beneath the surface. "Surely, there must be something you can tell me. I've uncovered some rather disturbing accounts in the library, and I would appreciate any insight you might have."

The room fell silent, the villagers avoiding eye contact with Richard as they sipped their tea. It was clear they had no intention of discussing anything with him.

"Very well," Richard conceded, his voice tense but controlled. "Thank you for your time."

He returned to his tea, his mind racing with thoughts of the grove and its secrets. Their silence only served to strengthen his resolve, reinforcing his determination.

"Let them keep their secrets," Richard thought, his eyes narrowing as he took another sip. "I will find the answers I seek, even if I must do so alone."

Richard's frustration gave way to a renewed sense of purpose as the villagers continued their muted conversations. He knew he was on the cusp of something significant that could potentially change everything he thought he knew about this quiet coastal village.

"I will not be deterred," Richard murmured under his breath, his fingers tightening around his teacup.

Richard pushed open the door to the library, his mind still racing from his fruitless conversation with the villagers. The room's quiet embraced him like a familiar friend; he had always found solace in books and research.

Among these dusty tomes and weathered pages lay the key to unlocking the secrets that haunted this village, and he felt a spark of hope ignite within him.

He resumed his research with renewed vigour, poring over ancient texts and yellowed newspaper clippings and village pamphlets. His fingers traced lines of text, eyes darting back and forth as he consumed every morsel of information he could find. Richard's determination to uncover the truth was palpable, each discovery feeding his growing obsession.

"Curse their silence," he muttered under his breath. "I'll piece together this puzzle without them."

Richard stepped back from the table as the clock struck noon, his hands trembling slightly from the adrenaline coursing through his veins. He had gathered an impressive array of notes detailing chilling tales of abductions, suicides, whispers of unexplained rituals, and even sacrifices. But there remained gaps in the narrative, pieces of the puzzle that eluded him.

Retiring to his room for lunch, Richard mulled over his findings as he absentmindedly picked at the cold meat and cheese laid out on his plate. His thoughts raced in circles, the weight of the dark history he had uncovered pressing down upon him. Richard knew that he would have to choose his next steps carefully. Would he seek out other sources of information? Or confront the villagers again, demanding the truth they so stubbornly withheld?

"Damn it all," he sighed, rubbing his temples as he tried to clear his thoughts. "What am I missing?"

Laying out his notes on the desk, Richard began to organize his findings, attempting to weave together a coherent story from the disparate threads of information he had gathered. The task was daunting, but he refused to let it overwhelm him. He was an educated man, a scholar whose entire professional life had been spent solving complex riddles and navigating knotty situations.

"Think, Richard," he murmured, his brow furrowed in concentration. "You have the pieces; now you just need to find how they fit together."

The minutes ticked by as Richard shuffled through his papers, rearranging them into different configurations, seeking the pattern that would reveal the truth beneath the chaos.

"By God," he whispered, a smile playing at the corners of his mouth as he felt the first glimmers of understanding begin to take shape. "I think I could have it."

"St. Saviour's," he whispered to himself, the name of the local church that had repeatedly cropped up in his research. That was where he might find the answers he sought; where the threads of the story could come together.

"Besides," he thought, "it's only logical to consult the church records for more information."

As he gathered his papers and tucked them neatly into a leather folio, Richard couldn't help but feel a pang of guilt for allowing his scientific curiosity to overshadow his original task. He knew full well that his investigation was straying beyond the scope of his assessment and evaluation of potential defensive sites. Still, the pull of the mystery was too strong to resist.

"Perhaps there's something to be learned here after all," he reasoned, trying to justify his actions. "Something that could benefit my work with the Directorate of Fortifications and Works in the long run."

With a resolute nod, Richard donned his hat and jacket, stepping out of the warm confines of his room and into the cool, dimly lit hallway. As he made his way down the stairs and to the front door, he felt the watchful gaze of the villagers upon him, their whispered conversations pausing as he approached, then resuming once he had passed.

"Let them talk," he thought defiantly. "I'll uncover the truth, no matter what they think."

Emerging from the inn, Richard took a deep breath of fresh air, expelling the decades-old library dust and feeling a renewed sense of purpose as he set off towards St. Saviour's.

The centuries-old stone church loomed ahead, its spire piercing the sky like a needle. It was an imposing sight, and Richard felt drawn to it, compelled by the knowledge of what might be hidden within its walls.

Passing through the lychgate and approaching the heavy wooden door, Richard hesitated momentarily, struck by an inexplicable sense of foreboding. He shook off the feeling with an impatient scoff, reminding himself that he was not a superstitious man.

"Come on, old chap," he muttered under his breath. "You've come this far."

With a determined push, he swung open the door and stepped inside. The air was cool and musty, the silence broken only by the creaking of ancient door hinges. He squinted in the dim light, making out rows of antique wooden pews and the gleaming glint of stained-glass windows.

"Right," he thought, steeling himself for the task at hand. "Time to find what I came for."

Chapter Six

Manuscripts of
Mystery.

R ichard closed the heavy door of St. Saviour's church, its hinges creaking once more as if protesting his intrusion into the ancient domain. Richard stepped down from the inner porch onto the time-worn stone flooring, his footsteps echoing as he marvelled at the centuries-old architecture. The weight of history pressed upon him as though the very stones were whispering tales of times long past.

As his eyes adjusted to the light filtering through stained glass windows, he noticed a middle-aged man near the altar, dressed in the sombre vestments of a vicar. The man regarded Richard with a stern expression that seemed etched into his features by years of tending to the spiritual needs of a secretive village.

"Good afternoon," Richard said, approaching the vicar with a respectful nod. "I am Captain Richard Headley."

"Captain Headley," the vicar replied, his voice betraying no warmth or curiosity. "What brings you to our humble church? Surely, the Germans haven't invaded us yet."

Richard hesitated, not wishing to alienate the vicar by responding with an equally tart comment; he was nonetheless unsure how much he should reveal about his true purpose. Opting for a partial truth, he said, "I'm in the area on behalf of the War Office and find myself with some spare time on my hands."

Richard involuntarily raised his hand to shield his eyes from the direct light streaming through the stained-glass window, at which point the vicar raised his hand to his head as if about to salute Richard, then realising his mistake he feigned a scratch behind an ear.

Lowering his hand, Richard smiled. The vicar did not.

"Vicar," Richard began, choosing his words carefully, "I have been researching the history of Hindringham Novers and its folklore. I believe the church records may hold valuable information to help me understand the village's past."

The vicar's eyebrows knitted together as his flushed cheeks returned to normal, yet his suspicion was palpable, a hint of irritation in his gaze. "Captain Headley, our church records are not for idle curiosity or entertainment. They serve as a testament to the faith and devotion of our parish over the centuries."

Richard understood the vicar's protectiveness but believed his cause was justified. "I assure you that my interest is sincere. I am a scholar by nature and have travelled here from Cambridge, and I can furthermore assure you that I will treat the knowledge contained within those records with the utmost respect."

"Also, vicar," he paused, hoping to appeal to the vicar's sense of duty. "Understanding the village's history and traditions might prove useful in my work here on behalf of the government."

Although his expression remained guarded, the vicar seemed to weigh Richard's words. Finally, with a sigh, he said, "Very well. Follow me."

With that, the two men made their way deeper into the church, leaving the sunlight behind them and descending into the shadows of history.

Moving through the dimly lit aisles of the church, Richard couldn't help but feel a growing sense of anticipation. The ancient stones, worn smooth by countless generations, seemed like they would whisper secrets to those who might listen closely enough. He admired the intricate stained-glass window, its vibrant colours casting a kaleidoscope of light across the floor.

The vicar led Richard to a small door tucked away behind the altar, its unassuming presence easily overlooked. As the door creaked open, a waft of musty air greeted them, carrying the scent of decaying parchment and age-old ink. The room beyond was cramped, with shelves lined with dusty books and ancient manuscripts stretching from floor to ceiling, illuminated by the light filtering through a single narrow window.

"Here are the church records," the vicar said, gesturing to the cluttered space. "Please, be careful with these fragile documents. And remember, Captain Headley, the knowledge you seek may not always bring comfort or understanding."

Richard nodded, hiding his surprise at how alike the villagers' warnings this one from the vicar sounded.

His mind was already racing ahead with possibilities as he surveyed the room; Richard knew the information he might unearth in this room could be as harrowing as that he had already discovered in the Black Shuck Inn library.

With a determined breath, driven by an unshakable need for clarity, he stepped into the dim confines of the archives, ready to delve into more of the shadowy recesses of Hindringham Novers' past.

The creaking of the ancient floorboards seemed magnified in the cramped room as Richard moved between shelves and bookcases, carefully examining the records, each page more delicate and brittle than the last. The air was heavy with the weight of centuries, the dim light barely enough to illuminate the faded ink on parchment. Richard's fingers moved gingerly, turning pages with the utmost care, his eyes scanning each line for any mention of the grove or the dark legacy he was now sure was associated with it.

One hour became two; two drifted into three. The room seemed to close in around Richard, shadows dancing across the walls and the musty scent almost suffocating. Eyes tired and back aching from the lack of any cushion on the hard and uncomfortable chair, Richard was about to call a halt on his endeavours.

Then, as if the records and archives understood they were about to be put aside, Richard elbowed a ledger he had previously discounted. Stooping to pick it up from the brick paviour floor, he glanced over the page it had fallen open on, a short list of book numbers corresponding to one of the bookcases in the corner he had yet to examine.

Richard could reach the bookcase without rising from the chair, and although the afternoon light was fading, he could still read the book spines. The three that stood out were those without titles, only Roman numerals: III, IV, and VII, an incomplete set of whatever information they contained. Nonetheless, he was suitably intrigued to make this his last effort at finding any information.

As he opened the first book and flicked through the pages, Richard's tiredness left him as he read references and accounts of "pagan woods" and "trees emanating evil energy" written in old, barely legible script. The words came alive from the page, sending a chill down his spine as he read them.

Through sheer persistence and a keen eye for detail, Richard had finally stumbled upon what he had been searching for.

Over the next hour, the three volumes led him to accounts scattered throughout the church records, painting a haunting picture of the grove's history and the broader history of Hindringham Novers. They spoke of strange rituals performed under a moonless sky and whispers of terrible deeds carried out in the name of ancient gods long forgotten. The oaks were described as twisted and contorted, their gnarled roots hiding the remnants of unholy offerings. Each account added another layer to the sense of mystery and unease surrounding the grove.

Richard couldn't help but feel a growing excitement as he continued to uncover more details about the village's dark past. He knew many would dismiss these tales as mere superstition, the product of fearful minds seeking meaning in the unknown. But Richard sensed something deeper within these stories, an unsettling truth hidden beneath layers of myth and legend. As he delved further into the records, a sense of foreboding grew within him, a nagging feeling that he was unearthing something best left undisturbed.

Despite the vicar's warning, Richard pressed on, his scholarly curiosity and need for answers pushing him deeper into Hindringham Novers secrets.

The dimming light of the late afternoon sun filtered through the small window, casting eerie shadows on the worn stone walls and heavily patinated wooden shelves and furniture. As Richard pored over the ancient manuscripts in the small, secluded room, he felt a strange sense of both excitement and unease, surrounded by centuries of history, each page holding secrets waiting to be unearthed.

"Ah, here we are," Richard murmured, his eyes widening as he found a passage detailing yet another chilling account of the grove. The old, faded ink seemed to pulse with energy as if the words held some ancient power. Richard could almost hear the whispers of those who had written these tales long ago, urging him to delve deeper into the darkness that shrouded the village. He continued scribbling notes in his notebook, the pen scratching across the paper in his haste to record every detail.

"Captain Headley," the vicar's voice suddenly cut through the silence, startling Richard out of his intense focus. He looked up to see the stern-faced cleric standing in the doorway, arms crossed, and a deep frown etched on his features. "I must insist that you've seen enough. It's time to leave this place."

Richard frowned, looking down at the parchment before him. He wasn't finished—not by a long shot. There were still countless pages to examine, and he couldn't shake the feeling that he was on the cusp of a significant breakthrough. But the vicar's impatience was palpable, and Richard knew better than to push his luck.

"Very well," he said reluctantly, closing the heavy tome with a soft thud. He gathered his notes and brushed the dust from his trousers. "Thank you for allowing me access to these records. They've been most . . . enlightening."

The vicar merely grunted in response, seemingly uninterested in the specifics of Richard's research, and then hovered with impatience as Richard replaced the books on their shelves. That done, he ushered Richard from the small room and through the church, the silence between them heavy and uncomfortable.

Reaching the entrance, Richard paused momentarily, glancing back at the shadowy corners of the ancient building. There was so much more to learn about Hindringham Novers and its mysterious grove; he could sense it like an itch under his skin. But for now, it seemed, he would have to be content with the knowledge he had already gained—and the tantalising thought of where that knowledge might lead him.

Richard's persistence had led him to the ancient manuscripts and records of St. Saviour's Church, where he now stood with the stern-faced vicar, who seemed eager for Richard to leave.

"Good day, Captain," the vicar said curtly, as he reached for the large ornate door handle.

"Vicar," Richard interjected tentatively, trying to maintain a polite tone despite his growing frustration at being unceremoniously ejected from the building, "there must be more to this village's history - something beyond what I found in your archives."

The vicar regarded him with narrowed eyes, his expression unyielding. "You've seen enough, Captain Headley. It's not our place to dig up the past."

"Surely you must have some insights or knowledge about the village and its surrounding area that isn't written down in the church records," Richard pressed, unwilling to let his curiosity go unsatisfied.

"Captain," the vicar replied, his voice cold and clipped, "I cannot help you further. Some things are best left alone, and I suggest that in this instance – that's what you do."

Richard clenched his jaw, sensing he would get no further assistance from the vicar. Disappointed but undeterred, he nodded and said, "Very well. I appreciate your time and allowing me access to your archives."

The vicar merely inclined his head, remaining silent as they exited the church. As Richard returned to the village, the sun dipped lower in the sky, casting a warm golden glow over the landscape. He couldn't help but feel a pang of disappointment in the face of the vicar's obstinance.

Yet, as he approached the Black Shuck Inn, thoughts of his discoveries swirled around his mind, refusing to be silenced, whispering tales of bygone days and lives long past. The villagers may have been tight-lipped and secretive, but there was no denying the truth hidden within the records he had discovered. And Richard was determined to uncover it, no matter where that path might lead him.

Pausing for a moment, he steeled himself against the lingering sense of foreboding before pushing open the heavy wooden door to The Black Shuck Inn.

Chapter Seven

Reluctant Revelations.

Richard entered the bar, brushing off the chill, inadvertently letting the door slam in the frame. Before returning to their hushed conversations, the patrons glanced briefly at the newcomer, who had allowed a gust of chilly wind to invade their warm haven. The fire flickered in the hearth, casting ominous shadows on the walls, deepening the mystery that clung to every corner of Hindringham Novers.

Richard's eyes scanned the room, resting on a solitary figure nursing his ale by the fire, the carpenter he had seen earlier in the day, effecting repairs to the timber frame of one of the houses a short distance from the Black Shuck Inn. A middle-aged man with a world-weary look about him, Richard recalled the advertising board the tradesman had propped up outside the house he'd been working on, claiming that he had over twenty-five years' experience working in the area.

Richard decided to take the opportunity to engage him in conversation as he probably knew as much as most, and more than some, about the village and its secrets.

"Good evening," Richard said, extending his hand in greeting as he approached the man. "I'm Captain Richard Headley – I'm staying in the inn. I believe we haven't had the pleasure of meeting yet."

The man looked up from his drink, his eyes narrowing as he assessed the stranger before him. "Evening," he replied cautiously, accepting Richard's handshake. "Alfred Harris. And you're right—we haven't met."

"May I join you?" Richard asked, gesturing to the empty chair beside Alfred.

"By all means," Alfred replied, waving him into the seat.

As Richard settled into the worn, wooden chair, he couldn't help but feel a sense of anticipation mingling with the unease that had plagued him since arriving in the village. He surmised that if anyone could shed light on the mysteries surrounding the village, the area, and possibly the grove, it would be someone who had worked here for many years. But how to broach the subject without raising suspicions?

"Beautiful village you have here," Richard began, watching as the firelight danced across the polished surface of his glass of ale. "And much of it down to your handiwork, I'd wager."

"Thank you," Alfred replied, taking a long swig and then wiping his mouth on his sleeve. "We like to think it's a special place. Not many outsiders come through, though."

"Indeed?" Richard replied, feigning casual interest. "Be that as it may, I must say that I find the village's history quite fascinating."

Richard felt a flicker of unease ripple through Alfred's demeanour as he spoke the words. It was subtle but unmistakable—the tightening of his grip on the glass, the slight shift in his posture. It appeared that Richard had struck upon a topic of interest.

"History, eh?" Alfred said with a small smile, his eyes shifting from the fire to meet Richard's gaze. "We have our fair share of tales and legends around these parts."

Richard leaned in, eager to hear more. "I'm something of a scholar myself," he confessed. "And I've been trying to learn more about the local folklore, particularly concerning the grove of oaks on the hill."

Alfred's expression darkened at the mention of the grove, and Richard knew that he had touched on a subject that held both power and fear for Alfred – as it did for all of the villagers. He also realized that if he pushed too hard, Alfred might withdraw entirely.

"Do you know much about the grove?" Richard casually asked, taking a sip of ale to mask his rising anxiety.

Alfred hesitated, his eyes flickering back to the fire as if seeking solace in its warmth. "I know some things," he admitted quietly. "But it's not a place we talk about much."

"Really?" Richard feigned surprise. "I'd love to hear what you know, purely as it relates to my interest in the area. I promise I won't pry into anything you don't wish to discuss."

For a moment, Alfred considered Richard's request. Then, with a deep breath, he began to speak, his voice barely audible above the crackling of the fire. Richard listened intently as the shadows played across the walls of the inn, his heart pounding with a mix of fear and excitement, knowing that he might very well be on the verge of unlocking some of the secrets that lay at the heart of Hindringham Novers.

The fire crackled, casting warm, flickering light across the inn's low-beamed ceiling. Richard watched Alfred take a slow sip of his ale, noting how the man seemed to relax slightly in response to their conversation. The villagers' wariness still lingered, but Richard had undoubtedly progressed with Alfred.

"Let me buy us another round," Richard suggested, gesturing to their near-empty glasses. "I find myself enjoying this talk of local history."

"Very kind of you, Captain," Alfred replied, his eyes lighting up with genuine appreciation. "I must say it's been a while since I've had such an interesting chat. After a full day's work in the village, I tend to find that I don't often want to mix with others."

As Richard made his way to the bar, he couldn't help but feel a sense of accomplishment. He was starting to gain Alfred's trust and, with it, a chance to unlock more of the village's secrets. As he waited for the innkeeper to fill their glasses, he reminded himself to remain focused on his task – he was here, after all, at the behest of the War Department. It wouldn't do to get carried away with his scholarly interests.

"Here we are, then," Richard said, returning to the table and setting the frothy pints before them. "To new friends and old stories."

"Cheers to that," Alfred agreed, clinking his glass against Richard's.

Richard steered the conversation back to Alfred's childhood with the new round of drinks providing a comfortable buffer. "You mentioned you grew up nearby," he said. "What was it like growing up in this beautiful countryside?"

Alfred took a thoughtful sip of ale, his face softening as he delved into memories long past. "Aye, it was a simpler time, for sure. We'd spend our days exploring the fields and woods, getting into all sorts of mischief."

"Any particular adventures come to mind?" Richard asked, feigning casual interest while keeping a keen eye on Alfred's reaction.

Alfred smiled, his eyes taking on a distant look. "Well, now that you mention it, there was this one time when we—my friends and I . . . and I had to drag them with me," he chuckled, "decided to explore the old mill by the river. It had been abandoned for years, and all sorts of stories had sprung up about haunted happenings and strange noises."

"Did you find anything unusual?" Richard prodded gently, not wanting to betray his anticipation.

"Nothing more than some rusty machinery and a few startled rats," Alfred admitted with a wry grin. "But the thrill of it, the feeling that we were delving into something forbidden . . . that stuck with me."

At that moment, Richard felt an unexpected kinship with Alfred. They shared a curiosity that drove them to seek answers, even when others wished to keep the truth hidden or were too afraid to become involved. As they continued their conversation, Richard hoped this connection would help him uncover the secrets of the grove and the village that guarded it so fiercely.

Richard and Alfred sipped their ales, for all the world, appearing like two old friends enjoying a once-a-week get-together. The warmth of the hearth and the alcohol had loosened their tongues, but Richard knew that he needed to approach the subject of the grove carefully or risk losing Alfred's trust.

"Speaking of your childhood adventures," Richard began, his voice casual and relaxed, "I've heard some interesting tales about the area . . . and, as I mentioned earlier, particularly about the grove on the outskirts of town. It seems to have quite the mysterious reputation."

Alfred's eyes narrowed slightly as if trying to read Richard's intentions. He swirled his ale in its mug before answering. "Aye, many stories are told about that place – some more far-fetched than others. People here tend to be wary of it."

"Really?" Richard feigned mild surprise while looking for signs of discomfort in his drinking companion. "What sort of things have you heard?"

"Ah, just the usual ghost stories and tales of strange sightings," Alfred replied, clearly downplaying the subject. "But then again, every village has a place like that, right? A spot where people claim to see and hear things they can't explain."

"True enough," Richard agreed, nodding thoughtfully. "But I'm always fascinated by local legends. They often contain a kernel of truth, even if it's buried deep beneath layers of myth and superstition." Despite the air of nonchalance he projected, Richard's mind raced with possibilities, searching for the best way to broach the question he truly wanted to ask.

"Have you ever witnessed anything strange or experienced anything you couldn't rationally explain in the grove, Alfred?" Richard asked, his tone light and purposefully offhand. Inwardly, he braced himself for the response, knowing that this was the moment when Alfred might either close off entirely or reveal information critical to Richard's understanding of the village's secrets.

Alfred stared into the fire for the briefest of moments before answering – his voice subdued. "Well, I can't say I've seen anything that natural causes or an overactive imagination couldn't explain away. But then again, I haven't spent much time in the grove since I was a boy."

"Ah, I see." Richard allowed the conversation to lapse momentarily, giving Alfred time to process the topic. He nursed his ale, contemplating his next move and hoping his persistence would eventually pay off.

Alfred moved to one side as the innkeeper carefully placed another log on the fire, which immediately crackled and hissed in the hearth. As the flames caught, Richard noticed an imperceptible exchange between the two of them – nothing more than a side glance at each other.

In the flickering light from the fire, Alfred's face, previously animated as he had recounted his childhood escapades, suddenly went rigid, his eyes narrowing with suspicion. The innkeeper continued his duties as he collected glasses from the nearby tables. When he was a sufficient distance, Alfred shifted in his seat, twisting his chair away from the other villagers who lingered in the room, each lost in their own little world as they eeked out their drinks.

"Look," Alfred said cautiously, "I don't know what you're after, but there are some things we just don't talk about around here." His voice dropped to a near-whisper, laced with a hint of fear that Richard hadn't noticed before.

Richard leaned in closer, lowering his voice to match Alfred's, creating an unintentional conspiratorial atmosphere between them. He looked directly into Alfred's eyes, trying to convey genuine interest and trustworthiness. "I understand your caution, Alfred. But I'm not interested in spreading gossip or stirring up trouble. You see, I'm a scholar by nature, and I've always been drawn to unravelling mysteries. And it seems to me, that this village has its fair share of them."

Alfred hesitated, glancing around the room again to ensure no one was eavesdropping. The tension in his shoulders eased ever so slightly, and Richard could see the struggle in his expression as he weighed whether to confide in him.

"Alright," Alfred whispered, leaning in even closer. "But you must promise never to speak of this to anyone else. What I'm about to tell you, well, it's something I've tried to forget for years. And I wouldn't want any harm to come to the people I care about around here because of my foolish decision to share it."

Richard nodded solemnly; his curiosity piqued. "You have my word, Alfred. Your secret will be safe with me."

With that assurance, Alfred took a deep breath and recounted his experiences, the words tumbling out, hushed and fearful.

"Alright," Alfred whispered, leaning in even closer. "It was when I was just a lad, no more than ten – maybe twelve – years old. My friends and I would sneak out at night and explore the countryside, as boys do. One evening, we saw lights in the grove."

He paused, swallowing hard, and Richard saw a sheen forming on his brow. "We didn't mean any harm, you understand. We were just curious about the place – since everyone seemed so keen on avoiding it."

"Of course," Richard murmured, urging him on with a nod.

"Anyway," Alfred continued, his voice hard for Richard to hear over the crackling fire. "We saw people there, dressed in strange robes, chanting in some heathen tongue we couldn't understand. It was like nothing we'd ever heard before. They were performing some kind of ritual—dancing around a great bonfire, their faces hidden by masks."

Alfred shuddered, and Richard could sense the fear that still haunted him all these years later. He pressed on gently, asking, "Did you ever see anything like that again?"

"No!" Alfred snapped, shaking his head. "No, we never went back after that night. But sometimes, when the moon is full, I hear whispers from others who've seen things they can't explain. And it's not just my generation; my father once told me stories about friends of his who had seen the same, and about his own father likewise."

The revelation sent a chill down Richard's spine, and he fought the urge to look over his shoulder at the innkeeper and the other patrons whose eyes he could feel boring into the back of his head. Instead, he focused on Alfred, trying to maintain his rationality. "Do you know who those people might have been? And what they were doing?"

Alfred hesitated, his gaze flitting toward the window. "I couldn't say for certain. Some folks around here claim they're remnants of an ancient pagan sect practising their rituals in secret. Others say they're something darker, more sinister."

"Whoever they are," he added, his voice barely above a whisper, "I wouldn't want to cross them."

Richard absorbed the information, his mind racing as he considered the implications of Alfred's story. It was becoming increasingly clear that there was much more to this village and its mysterious grove than met the eye—and he was determined to fathom it out.

"Thank you for telling me, Alfred," Richard said sincerely. "I know how difficult it must have been for you to recount such an experience. But please be rest assured, your secret is safe with me."

The dying embers of the fire cast flickering shadows across the inn's emptying bar as a few remaining patrons whispered and exchanged glances before leaving for the night. Richard watched Alfred, who had grown quiet after sharing his childhood experiences, his hands gripping his near-empty tankard with white knuckles.

"Alfred," Richard began carefully, "I have a proposition for you." The older man looked up, his eyes guarded but curious. "Why don't we visit the grove together? It might help to confront your old memories in the light of day."

Alfred scoffed, shaking his head as he rose from his chair. "No, Captain. I've done my best to avoid that place all these years. I won't go back now."

"Please, hear me out," Richard urged, standing and placing a calming hand on Alfred's shoulder. He could feel the tension in the man's muscles as though he were ready to flee at any moment. "You've carried this burden alone for too long. Let me join you in facing it. Together, we may uncover something important about the village's past that may give you peace."

Alfred hesitated, his gaze darting between Richard's earnest expression and the door leading into the cold night outside. His chest heaved with anxious breaths, his mind wrestling with the idea of returning to the source of his nightmares.

"Alfred," Richard continued softly, leaning closer to speak directly into his ear, "you're not alone anymore. Trust me."

For a moment, silence filled the space between them, broken only by the crackling remnants of the fire. Then, slowly, Alfred nodded, his eyes filling with a mixture of fear and determination.

"Alright, Captain," Alfred nodded, looking visibly relieved as he reached for his tankard and drained the last of his ale. "Just promise me something, Captain... we must be careful. There are things we can't begin to understand in this world, and sometimes it's best to let sleeping dogs lie."

"I'll keep that in mind," Richard replied, his thoughts already consumed by the puzzle before him.

"Then we'll go tomorrow night," Alfred said, eyes downcast. "It's a full moon, so we shouldn't need lanterns. And anyways, it's said around these here parts, that's when the grove is most . . . alive."

"Very well," Richard agreed, although the mention of the full moon sent a shiver down his spine.

"Meet me outside after sunset," Alfred instructed his voice barely a whisper over the crackling fire. "And come prepared for anything, Captain."

"Understood." Richard nodded, feeling the weight of the decision, settling on them both. He couldn't ignore the tension in the air, the sense that they were about to cross a threshold from which there would be no return.

"Thank you, Alfred," Richard added, firmly clasping the older man's shoulder. "I know this isn't easy for you, but I believe it's important – to us both."

Alfred looked up, meeting Richard's gaze with fear and determination. "I just hope we don't regret it, Captain."

As he excused himself to retire for the night, Richard couldn't help but feel a mixture of conflicting emotions for what lay ahead. For better or worse, the mystery of Hindringham Novers had ensnared him—and there was no turning back now.

Having parted ways with Alfred, Richard retreated upstairs to the sanctuary of his room. As he climbed the creaky wooden stairs, the anticipation and trepidation that had taken root within him grew heavier with each step. He couldn't help but feel a sense of impending doom as if some nameless force were watching him from the shadows.

"Focus, old man," Richard whispered, attempting to steady his racing thoughts.

He reached his door, fumbling with the key before finally unlocking it. The dim light of the room seemed darker than usual, casting eerie, distorted shapes upon the walls. Richard quickly lit two more candles, hoping to banish the creeping unease threatening his resolve.

"Tomorrow night will reveal the truth," he muttered, pacing the small space. "There must be a rational explanation for all this."

As Richard prepared for bed, he couldn't help but dwell on the tales of the strange occurrences that Alfred had shared, what sounded to him like generations of repeated ancient druid-type rituals. The fear in the older man's eyes had been palpable, and despite Richard's best efforts to remain logical, it struck a chord deep within him.

The wind outside howled mournfully, rattling the windowpanes and heightening the oppressive atmosphere. Richard recalled memories of his academic days at Kings College, seeking solace in the familiar world of reason and logic.

Despite the doubts that still gnawed at the edges of his consciousness, Richard knew that understanding the truth about the grove would ultimately give him control over his growing fear.

Climbing into the narrow bed, he reminded himself of his father's words, "Knowledge is the key."

With those words echoing through his thoughts, Richard finally drifted off to sleep, one hand gripping the edge of the bed as if bracing himself for the unknown that awaited him in the grove under the full moon's cold, unforgiving light.

Chapter Eight

Grove of Shadows.

The chill slowly subsided as the room warmed up from the sunlight filtering through the glass. Richard sat hunched over his desk, pen scratching furiously on the note paper as he meticulously wrote up his notes from the previous day's research in the inn's library and at St. Saviour's church. He couldn't help but feel a sense of excitement yet unease as he pieced together the village's dark past, the mysterious grove, and its connections to strange rituals, sacrifices, and missing villagers.

Around mid-morning, amidst his deep concentration, a soft knock on Richard's door startled him, breaking his reverie. He rose from his seat, opening it to find Alfred, the carpenter he had spoken with the previous evening. Alfred's eyes held an uneasy mixture of fear and determination.

"Captain, sir," he whispered, glancing nervously down the hallway. "I've been thinking about our conversation, and I must ask you to reconsider going to the grove tonight."

Richard studied the man before him, noting his clammy disposition and the slight tremble in his voice. He wondered if this was merely remnants of childhood fears or something more substantial.

"Alfred, I understand your concern," Richard gestured him into his room, his voice steady and reassuring. "But as a man of science and reason, I cannot ignore the opportunity to uncover the truth behind these legends and mysteries that have plagued this village for generations."

Alfred hesitated, clearly wrestling with his own emotions. "I know, sir," he said finally. "But I cannot shake the feeling that we're meddling in things beyond our understanding. Please, at least promise me we'll be cautious."

"Of course," Richard agreed, placing a hand on Alfred's shoulder. "We shall tread carefully, keeping our wits about us. And if we find ourselves in danger, we'll leave immediately."

Alfred nodded, the tension in his shoulders lessening slightly. "Very well, Captain. I shall meet you outside here tonight. May God protect us both." With that, he turned and left the room.

Richard couldn't help but feel the weight of Alfred's words as he closed the door behind him. He had always been a man who relied on logic and reason, but as the day wore on and evening drew nearer, he felt an unfamiliar sense of unease gnawing at the edge of his thoughts.

As the sun dipped below the horizon, it cast a gloomy veil over the village of Hindringham Novers. The encroaching darkness seemed to amplify Richard's growing sense of unease, gnawing at the edge of his thoughts like a persistent shadow. He knew he couldn't ignore the opportunity to uncover the truth behind the mysterious grove and its dark history, even if it meant going against the villagers' warnings.

Gathering his courage, Richard left the inn and crossed the road to wait for Alfred, as arranged. The village had taken on an eerie quietness as if the air held its breath in anticipation of what would come.

"Captain Headley, sir," Alfred whispered with a tremble, emerging from the shadows beside a derelict barn. "Are you ready for this?"

Richard nodded, betraying no hint of the apprehension clawing at his chest. "Yes, let's go."

They moved stealthily through the darkened village, avoiding any potential witnesses who might question their late-night excursion. Every creak and rustle seemed magnified tenfold, making Richard's heart race with adrenaline. He tried to focus on the logical reasons for his investigation instead of the ghostly legends that haunted the back of his mind.

"Remember, we must tread carefully," Richard whispered. "We know not what awaits us in the grove."

Alfred nodded, his eyes wide with fear. "Aye, Captain. I pray we find nothing more sinister than my foolish childhood memories."

As they crisscrossed the countryside, Richard couldn't help but feel the weight of Alfred's words bearing down upon him. He had always been a man who relied on logic and reason, but the closer they drew to the mysterious grove, the harder it became to maintain that rationality. The night seemed alive with shadows and country noises, playing tricks on his senses and threatening to pry open the door to a world of superstition he wasn't sure he was ready to pass through.

"Stay close," Richard instructed as they approached the grove's edge, its gnarled trees looming like ancient guardians. "We'll be in and out before anyone is the wiser."

With that, they stepped into the darkness, leaving the safety of reason behind them.

The full moon cast its eerie glow upon the ancient oaks, their contorted branches reaching out like skeletal fingers in the cold night air. Richard and Alfred stood at the edge of the grove, their breath visible as they hesitated momentarily before venturing further.

"Looks different under the moonlight," Richard observed, his voice barely concealing his unease. "I marked some trees earlier, but it seems our mysterious villagers have removed the chalk. They don't want us meddling here."

Alfred swallowed hard, his eyes darting nervously, still able to make out details under the bright moonlight. "Aye, sir. This place has haunted my dreams ever since I was a boy. That's where I saw the robed figures performing their rituals around the fire," he pointed ahead, indicating a small clearing in the trees some thirty yards distant.

His voice trembled as he recounted the memory, recalling the feeling of terror that had gripped him as a child. "I hid behind a tree, over there, watching them dance and chant in their unknown tongue. I couldn't make out their faces, but the sense of evil was all around. It was as if the very trees were alive with it."

Richard looked around, fighting the urge to let his imagination run wild; he needed to remain logical and rational despite the dark history he had uncovered about the village and the grove. He focused on Alfred's words and tried to analyse them from a scholarly perspective.

"Your account aligns with what I found in the church records," Richard said, forcing his thoughts back into the realm of reality.

"Ancient accounts spoke of 'pagan woods' and 'trees emanating evil energy.' But we mustn't let superstition rule our minds."

"Easy for you to say, sir," Alfred responded, his voice strained, betraying his fear. "You didn't grow up hearing the whispers, seeing the shadows in the corner. The things I saw here as a boy . . . they left their mark on me."

Richard placed a reassuring hand on Alfred's shoulder. "We'll face this together, Alfred. Let's see if we can uncover the truth behind these legends and bring some semblance of peace to this village . . . and you."

Together, they stepped deeper into the grove, their hearts pounding in unison as the shadows danced around them, merging with moonlight and memories.

"Perhaps the rituals you witnessed as a boy were remnants of ancient practices tied to this land," Richard whispered as they approached the clearing. "It could be that these ceremonies have left a lasting impact on the villagers' collective psyche."

"Maybe," Alfred replied hesitantly, "but there's something more to it, sir. Something . . . unnatural."

As they continued deeper into the grove, the full moon cast a haunting glow on the knotted and twisted oaks, heightening the sense of foreboding. A sudden chill raced down Richard's spine, making him shiver involuntarily.

"Did you feel that as well, sir?" Alfred asked, his voice wavering with fear.

"Yes . . . but I don't know what it was that I felt." Richard said, trying to maintain his composure. However, the unease was palpable, and he could not deny that the surroundings were affecting him.

"Them . . . them's what I felt," Alfred whispered, his eyes wide with terror as he raised his arm slowly and pointed towards the far edge of the clearing.

Ghostly figures materialised among the trees, their ethereal forms slowly advancing towards Richard and Alfred. The air around them grew colder, sending shivers down their spines. Richard recalled the notes he had made after his research in the library about missing villagers, unexplained deaths, suicide pacts, and sacrifices. He couldn't help but believe that he was witnessing evidence of these events in the images before him.

"Alfred," Richard said quietly, "do not panic. We must stay calm and rational. These . . . entities may be manifestations of the village's tragic past, but we cannot let our fear control us."

The ghostly figures drew closer, their features becoming more discernible. Richard felt his heart pounding as he struggled to remain composed. The duality of his military background and scholarly pursuits warred within him; the soldier urged him to retreat whilst the academic demanded answers.

"Sir," Alfred whispered urgently, "Captain, sir...I don't know if I can do this."

"Stay close to me," Richard commanded, determination etched on his face. He knew that facing these spectres would require all the strength and resolve they could muster.

As the ghostly figures continued to coalesce into more human-type shapes, Richard's rationality began to buckle under the weight of the terrifying scene unfolding before him. The spectral forms seemed to sense their fear, blocking every attempt at escape as if they were herding them deeper into the grove.

"Captain," Alfred whispered, his voice trembling with panic, "we can't stay here any longer. We need to find a way out!"

Richard's mind raced, recalling the notes he had made after his research in the church as he transcribed ancient accounts of 'pagan woods' and 'trees emanating evil energy.' He knew he had to maintain control of the situation, but his heart pounded, and fear threatened to overtake him.

"Stay close, Alfred," Richard said, his voice wavering despite his efforts to remain composed. "If we stick together, we'll find a way out."

As they cautiously moved through the grove, it felt as though the oppressive darkness was closing in around them, and the twisted tree limbs reached out like gnarled hands attempting to grasp them.

"Look!" Alfred cried suddenly, pointing to a gap where several eerie shapes had merged into one. "There's an opening – we have to move quickly!"

Without hesitation, they dashed towards the gap, narrowly avoiding the grasping tendrils of the ghostly figures. As they broke free from the confines of the grove, they felt the oppressiveness immediately lift from them as though breaking the surface of a frozen lake from below.

They could see the village below them from their vantage point on the hill, rooftops bathed in the moonlight shimmering on the night-time dew.

"Keep going, Alfred!" Richard urged. "We must reach The Black Shuck Inn!"

Their breaths came in ragged gasps as they entered the village and raced down the empty streets, the sense of isolation and dread only intensifying their need for safety. The cobbles beneath their feet echoed their frantic footsteps, and the moonlit shadows seemed to twist and writhe around them.

"Captain," Alfred panted, his eyes wide with fear, "do you think they're following us?"

"Let's not wait to find out," Richard replied grimly, his mind still reeling from the horrifying events they had just faced.

Finally, they reached the familiar entrance of The Black Shuck Inn, practically collapsing through the door as they stumbled inside. For the moment, they were safe, but Richard felt sure that the haunting images of the ghostly figures would be etched in their minds for ever.

Gasping for breath, Richard and Alfred leaned against the worn wooden bar of The Black Shuck Inn, their hearts pounding. Their gazes darted to the window, half expecting the ghostly figures to emerge from the outside darkness. But the spirits hadn't pursued them, it seemed. The room was empty of patrons, and they could hear the innkeeper in the back room whistling; he would be through within moments as he no doubt heard the bell over the door ring.

"Are you alright, Alfred?" Richard asked, his voice tinged with concern.

"Y-yes," Alfred stammered, his eyes still wide with terror. "I think so. I will return home now, as it's only a few minutes from here."

"That's a good idea. I could do with getting to my room," Richard suggested, determined not to let the innkeeper witness their fear. He climbed the rickety staircase, each step sinking him deeper in thought, haunted by what he had seen.

Once inside his room, Richard splashed his face with water from the bowl on the nightstand and turned to face the window as he dried himself. His heart raced as his mind filled with thoughts of the restless spirits seeking justice or revenge. He couldn't shake the feeling that they were still watching him, somehow.

"Get a grip," he muttered under his breath, trying to centre himself. He knew he needed to act if he was to find any semblance of peace tonight.

Determined to protect himself from whatever malevolent forces lurked outside, Richard grabbed hold of the heavy wardrobe beside his bed. With adrenaline coursing through his veins, he used all his strength to shuffle it across the creaky floorboards, positioning it in front of the window. If anything tried to get in, it would have to make quite a racket to do so – and that would buy him precious time to react.

After securing the window, Richard sat on the edge of his bed, his hands trembling from the night's events. He stared at the door, contemplating whether he had done enough to keep the supernatural horrors at bay.

"Alfred saw them too," he whispered, seeking validation for his fears. "But we escaped . . . for now, at least."

His mind raced with the implications of Alfred's account, the chilling rituals, and the dark history he had uncovered. But for tonight, he had done what he could to ensure his safety. He needed to focus on the here and now and try to make sense of everything once dawn broke.

"Tomorrow," Richard murmured as he lay back on his bed, exhaustion finally taking over. "I'll face it all tomorrow."

The door to Richard's room creaked open, revealing the innkeeper's daughter, who carefully balanced a food tray. She cast a nervous glance at the wardrobe barricading the window before placing the tray on the small table by Richard's bed. "Father heard you come in earlier," she said. "He thought you may be hungry."

"Thank you," he muttered, still half-asleep, his voice betraying his exhaustion. Richard bolted the door as the girl left, contemplating his next move.

"Alfred saw them too," Richard reminded himself one more, finding solace in the fact that he wasn't alone in his experiences. He picked up the cold meat pie from the tray and took a bite, chewing mechanically while his mind churned with thoughts of spectres and dark histories. Then, setting the pie aside, Richard wedged a wooden chair under the doorknob, ensuring that no one – or no thing – could enter his sanctuary unannounced.

"Let them try," he thought defiantly. But as he lay down on the bed, his facade of courage crumbled, replaced by a gnawing anxiety. His heart pounded in his chest; each beat reminded him of the terror lurking amongst the trees on the hill.

"Damn this village and its secrets," he muttered, feeling an odd mix of dread and determination. He knew he couldn't leave Hindringham Novers without getting to the bottom of the mysteries that haunted it.

As Richard pulled the thin blanket over his trembling body, he tried to focus on his breathing, willing himself to find some semblance of peace amidst the chaos of his thoughts. He closed his eyes and listened to the wind picking up outside his barricaded window, imagining it carrying away the ghosts and shadows that had invaded his life.

"Tomorrow," he whispered, hoping daylight would bring clarity and reason. "I will face whatever comes, but tonight . . . I need to sleep tonight."

The rhythmic sound of his breaths gradually lulled Richard into a fitful slumber, where dreams of ghostly figures and ancient rituals wove a terrifying tapestry.

Chapter Nine

Waking Nightmares.

The shrieking wind tore through the night, its howl ripping Richard from his uneasy slumber. Disoriented and fearful, he bolted upright in bed, heart pounding as if it sought to escape his chest. He wiped the cold sweat from his brow, trying to recall where he was.

"Focus, old chap," Richard muttered, his voice a dry rasp. The previous days' events came flooding back, and he knew he was still in Hindringham Novers, lodged in the eerily quaint Black Shuck Inn.

Desperate for some semblance of control, Richard reached for the candle on the bedside table, his hands shaking as he fumbled with the matches. After several failed attempts, the candle finally lit, casting a flickering glow across the room that danced with shadows like some out-of-time waltz.

"Damn this place," he whispered, willing his heart to slow its frantic pace. As an educated man, he clung to logic, but something about the village and its secrets gnawed at the edges of his reason. He couldn't shake the feeling that he was caught in a web of darkness, waiting for some unseen force to close in and consume him.

The unearthly moans resonated through Richard's room. He shivered, the sound sending goosebumps down his spine. "Mother of God, what is that?" he thought, trying to rationalise what he was hearing.

"Get a grip," he whispered, though it did little to calm his nerves. "It must be the wind playing tricks on me or perhaps an animal outside," he thought. Yet, as he tried to convince himself of these reasonable explanations, his mind wandered back to the ghostly figures he had witnessed only hours before.

Richard was now even more sure that the notes he had made following his visit to the inn's library and the church archives had influenced his normal rational train of thought. His discovery of stories about unexplained deaths, missing villagers, sacrifices, and suicides impacted his increasingly fragile state of mind.

In the darkness of his mind, shutting his eyes tightly, Richard could still see the ethereal, ghostly shapes swirling around Alfred and himself, the spectres that had coalesced into near-human forms.

Opening his eyes with a start, Richard, bit by bit, focussed on a mistiness forming in the gloom on the far side of the room. Swirling in the gradually thickening vapour, he could make out shapes, forming slowly but recognisably into... what? Spectres? Ghosts? Spirits?

He couldn't help but believe that he was witnessing evidence of the earlier events in the grove, in the apparitions before him.

Were they real, or had they been conjured by his memories, these ghostly figures that began to materialise around him?

As he sat on his bed, knees pulled up tight to his chest, Richard could now see the ghosts – for what else were they – pass directly through the walls and ceiling and then back into his room again as if seeking their prey.

Their ill-defined yet pale, contorted faces filled with anguish, their eyes hollow and desperate. Richard felt his breath hitch, terror constricting his chest.

"Stay away!" Richard choked out, his voice barely audible, his throat dry with fear. The apparitions paid no heed to his plea, drifting closer as if attracted by his trepidation.

Richard's rationality crumbled beneath the weight of his terror, leaving only frantic thoughts clawing at the corners of his mind. Was this another manifestation of the grove's malevolence? Were these the spirits of villagers who had fallen prey to its darkness?

"Please . . . I don't want any harm . . ." he managed to stammer, but the words seemed not to affect the spectral figures. Their mournful wails grew louder, echoing through the small room until it felt like his head would split open.

"Stop it! Just stop!" Richard cried out, his fists clenched, his heart pounding like a drummer in his chest. But the ghosts refused to relent, their cries drilling into his very being.

The flickering candlelight cast elongated shadows on Richard's bedroom walls as if the darkness were reaching out to him. He looked around desperately for something to defend himself with. His walking cane propped by the nightstand caught his eye, and without a second thought, he grabbed it, holding it in front of him like a makeshift sword.

"Stay back!" Richard shouted, his voice wavering with fear. Despite his officer training and acute analytical and academic mind, he couldn't help but feel terror coursing through his veins.

As the ghostly figures continued their relentless encircling, Richard knew in his heart that this was no enemy he could ever have envisioned facing; no tutelage in methods of combat could ever have prepared him for this onslaught; no logic he might muster could be applied to this situation.

"Damn you!" Richard yelled, swinging his cane at the nearest apparition. To his dismay, the weapon passed right through the figure as if it were thin air. He tried again with another spirit, and still, his efforts were futile. The realisation that he could not defend himself from these unearthly beings left him feeling even more helpless.

"Enough!" Richard roared, "You will not break me!"

Despite his determination, the ghostly figures remained undeterred, moving closer toward him. Their mournful cries continued to echo throughout the room, threatening to drown out any semblance of rationality or hope. Richard felt an overwhelming sense of despair washing over him as they drew nearer. It was as if the very essence of fear had gripped his heart, squeezing the life force from within him.

"Please," he whispered, his voice barely a whisper, "Someone . . . please." His plea seemed to fall on deaf ears, the ghostly figures continuing their swirling attack. Panic began to overtake him as he swung his cane fruitlessly, desperation gripping his every movement.

"Help me," Richard gasped, his voice cracking under the weight of his terror. "Someone . . . anyone . . . "But there was no one to hear his sobs or come to his aid. The spirits continued to surge around him, their cries growing more piercing, their presence suffocating.

The air seemed to grow colder and heavier as more spirits materialised, floating around Richard's bed like spectres of doom. Their pale, contorted faces twisted in anguish. The chilling atmosphere intensified, and Richard felt like he was drowning in a sea of terror.

"Leave me be!" Richard shouted, his voice wavering with desperation. He swatted at the ghostly figures, his movements becoming more frantic as their mournful cries drilled into his mind.

"Please . . . stop," he gasped between panicked breaths, but the spirits gave no heed to his pleas. Instead, they continued to circle the bed, a relentless storm of torment that threatened to shatter the last remnants of Richard's resolve.

Heaving with exertion, Richard tried to focus on the memories of his time at King's College, desperately seeking solace in the days when his life was guided by reason and logic. He clung to the hope that somehow, despite the terrifying events unfolding before him, there must be an explanation rooted in reality.

"Perhaps . . . it's all just . . . in my mind," Richard stammered, struggling to maintain a semblance of rationality amid the chaos. But even as he spoke the words, he knew deep down that no mere hallucination could ever conjure such vivid, visceral terror.

As the wailing spirits continued their haunting dance around him, Richard felt the weight of his own helplessness crushing down upon him. With each passing moment, the darkness encroaching upon his mind threatened to swallow him whole, leaving nothing behind but a hollow shell of the man he once was.

The ghostly figures in the room shifted, their ghastly features contorting into expressions of pain and despair. One by one, they pointed accusing fingers at Richard, their mouths gaping wide in silent screams that only intensified his terror.

Then, in the deepest recesses of his near-broken mind, Richard heard a weak, almost childlike voice seeming to call to him. Covering his ears and shutting his eyes tight, Richard tried to concentrate on this new yet equally terrifying experience.

As he focussed on the voice within his mind, Richard heard, "Let me sleep... please, just let me sleep." He immediately thought the words must be a manifestation of his own disjointed and terror-stricken thoughts. Removing his hands from his ears and opening his eyes, Richard heard the same, waif-like voice scream at him from within his skull.

"It's Rachel. Just let me sleep . . . please let me sleep."

"Wh-what do you want from me?" Richard screamed back at the voice within his mind.

With that, the spirits advanced upon him, more abhorrent than before, their cold, lifeless eyes boring into his very soul. Desperation clawed at Richard's mind, giving way to the raw, primal instinct for self-preservation. He fought to cling to logic, to reason, but every fibre of his being screamed for him to flee this unholy nightmare.

Pressing himself against the headboard as if it might offer some protection from the spectral threats surrounding him and struggling now to get more than a pitiful whimper to escape his trembling lips, Richard managed to stammer as he tried to beg for mercy, "Please . . . I didn't mean . . . "

But the sheer terror that gripped his every sinew rendered him incapable of forming a coherent sentence. As the spirits closed in, Richard found himself trapped between two warring factions within his psyche: the scholar who had faced life's challenges with unwavering determination and the vulnerable man who, for the first time in his life, had come face to face with the very embodiment of fear.

"Is this my punishment?" he thought frantically, recalling the villagers' warnings and the dark secrets he had uncovered within the library and the church in his relentless pursuit of knowledge. "Am I to pay for my misplaced curiosity with my sanity?"

And then, just as it seemed he would be overwhelmed entirely, a thought flickered, conjured from the remnants of rationality in Richard's mind. Though clouded by terror, it provided a single spark of hope - a fleeting image of St. Saviour's church, its ancient stones radiating a sense of timeless wisdom and strength.

"St. Saviour's . . . the church . . . there must be something more there," he thought, latching onto the idea as a lifeline. "The vicar didn't want me to continue my research... if I can just make it through this night, I'll find a way to end this, once and for all."

But the night was far from over, and the spirits' silent screams continued to echo in Richard's ears, their presence a constant reminder of the darkness lurking within the heart of Hindringham Novers and in the grove of ancient oaks on the hill. As he lay there, shivering in the cold embrace of terror, he knew that neither reason nor logic could keep the spectres from him.

"Help me, anybody... somebody," he whispered into the void, praying for a reprieve that seemed eternally out of reach.

"Please," he whispered hoarsely, his voice barely audible, "I only wanted to understand." But the spirits showed no mercy, their anguished screams echoing through the chamber like a mournful symphony.

"Damn you!" Richard yelled, tears streaming down his face as his rationality shattered under the weight of fear. He recalled the villagers' warnings, the old woman's cryptic words at the inn, and Alfred's insistence on leaving the grove's secrets alone. It seemed so painfully clear now, yet far too late to change his fate.

"Forgive me," he choked out, his body trembling uncontrollably. The spirits swirled around him, their chilling presence draining his soul's last remnants of warmth.

As the horrifying scene reached its crescendo, Richard's eyes widened with pure terror, his thoughts consumed by the dark history of Hindringham Novers as his once unshakable commitment to reason and logic was crushed under the unbearable burden of the supernatural, leaving him adrift in a sea of dread and despair.

And then, just as swiftly as it had begun, the room fell silent. Overwhelmed by the nightmarish ordeal, Richard's mind could bear no more. His consciousness slipped away, plummeting into the abyss as his body slumped against the headboard.

At that moment, Captain Richard Headley, who had arrived in the village with such confidence and determination, was lost to the shadows that haunted Hindringham Novers and temporarily swallowed up by the darkness he had so desperately sought to understand.

The room was steeped in an eerie silence as Richard's consciousness ebbed and flowed between nightmarish dreams and semi-lucid thoughts.

The once-present ghostly figures having vanished without a trace, the flickering candlelight cast elongated shadows across the walls, dancing in time with the diminishing howl of the wind outside.

"Was it real, or just a nightmare?" he wondered, during a period of wakefulness, fighting to stave off sleep lest the encroaching darkness should swallow him whole. But his body betrayed him, surrendering to the exhaustion that gnawed at every fibre of his being.

Waking again as the first light blinked over the vast open seascape to the east, Richard's thoughts immediately turned to trying to rationalise his situation. "Perhaps it was only my imagination, or the villagers have woven their superstitions so tightly around me that I've become ensnared in their web of fear."

As his mind drifted between wakefulness and sleep, Richard grappled with the tension between his rationality and the unease that had wormed its way into his thoughts. He wrestled with questions that seemed to have no answers, each pulling him further from the safety of logic.

"Can I truly disregard what I've seen and heard... even in the grove last night?" he asked, his heart pounding. "Or am I merely clinging to my scepticism for fear of admitting that forces beyond my understanding are at play here?"

His breath came in ragged gasps as he lay on his dishevelled bed, the weight of his thoughts threatening to crush him. And yet, he could not bring himself to abandon his quest for knowledge. If anything, the mysterious events of the past few days had only strengthened his resolve to uncover the truth.

"Today," he vowed, his voice cracking with emotion, "I will finish this, no matter what horrors may yet await me. I will complete my research at the church. And... I will find out who Rachel is."

With those words, he drew upon the last reserves of his strength and forced his eyes open, desperate to stay awake just a little longer. But it was a futile effort, for sleep had already claimed him, dragging him down into its suffocating embrace.

"Today," he whispered again as the darkness seeped in and swallowed him whole.

Chapter Ten

In the Face of Fear.

A cold sweat clung to Richard's skin as he slowly sat up in bed, feeling the weight of exhaustion pressing down upon him. Lingering fear from the previous night's events clouded his thoughts, making it difficult to distinguish between the nightmares that had plagued his dreams and the reality which awaited him outside his barricaded room.

With bleary eyes, Richard surveyed his surroundings. The remnants of his desperate attempts at protection lay scattered about the room: a wooden chair jammed under the door handle and the old, heavy wardrobe pushed against the window, its bulk blocking out most of the daylight that was starting to filter through. As rational as Richard tried to be, he couldn't deny the overwhelming dread that had taken hold of him last night. To think he would resort to such measures only emphasised the terror that had consumed him.

Shaking off the remaining tendrils of sleep, Richard swung his legs over the side of the bed, mustering the energy to stand, his limbs stiff with tension. He glanced again at the barricades he had constructed, a grim reminder of his vulnerability. Determination began to replace his lingering fear; he knew he must continue his research at the church to uncover the truth behind the haunting voice of Rachel and her connection to the dark legacy of the grove.

But first, he needed to face the morning and the villagers who undoubtedly whispered about him behind closed doors. Had they heard him last night? Nobody had come to his room to establish his wellbeing, all except the girl with the food tray.

It was still early, and he had not slept well for two nights, so Richard decided that an extra hour of sleep would do him no harm.

Distorted memories of eerie howls, swirling wind, and nightmarish apparitions haunted Richard's thoughts as he lay on the bed. Once more, the room seemed to close in, suffocating him with its oppressive atmosphere. Richard knew he couldn't allow himself to be paralysed by fear; to find solace in this village, he needed to confront the source of these horrors. The words spoken by the ghostly Rachel echoed through his mind: "Let me sleep." Was it a plea for peace or a warning?

Richard clenched his fists, determined to seek answers at St. Saviour's church. His rational side urged him to believe there was a logical explanation for the events he experienced. But deep down, the creeping tendrils of doubt and dread threatened to overpower him. Perhaps he could free himself from their torment if he could only decipher the truth behind the village's dark past and appease the spirits.

"Rachel," he whispered, the name resonating like a key to unlock the hidden mysteries of Hindringham Novers. His resolve strengthened, buoyed by the hope of finding clarity within the ancient church records.

"Whatever secrets are there, I will uncover them," his voice firm despite the slight quivering of his hands. "I won't allow myself to become another victim of this town's twisted legacy."

No matter how he tried, Richard could not fall back to sleep. With a deep breath, he rose and started dismantling the barricades that had offered him a temporary safe haven, steeling himself for whatever challenges lay ahead.

The cold stone walls of St. Saviour's church offered little comfort as Richard opened the heavy wooden door, its creaking echoing in the silence. A chill crept up his spine, but he pushed aside his unease, focusing on the task at hand.

"Good morning, Captain Headley," the vicar greeted him from just inside the doorway, eyeing him warily. "Back again so soon?"

Richard's suspicions toward the vicar had grown since they last met, but he knew that the answers he sought lay hidden within the ancient records stored in the church's dusty archives, so he must dance around his reservations towards the man.

"Indeed," replied Richard, his voice steady despite his turmoil. "I believe the church records may hold the key to understanding the . . . recent and curious happenings in this village."

"Recent and curious happenings? Oh dear, Captain, you do seem to be one for melodrama!" the vicar sighed in that way that only a vicar can sigh.

Richard couldn't reveal his true motives – finding answers about the haunting voice that might come from a spirit named Rachel – but he hoped the vicar would relent.

The vicar hesitated, his eyes narrowing, before reluctantly nodding. "Very well. But you must not take any records from the premises."

"Of course," Richard assured him. "Thank you, Vicar."

"You know the way to the archives," the vicar said as he picked up a small pile of hymn books, turning to leave – his cassock disturbing the dust on the floor around him.

Then, stopping and facing Richard, the vicar added, "I have the joy of attending a meeting of the Inter-Parish Great War Widows Group this morning and will be leaving here in a little over two hours. Please make sure that you have completed your research by then."

With that, he spun on the spot and flounced off towards the choir loft.

With time now of the essence, Richard headed straight for the archives, once more settling on the same uncomfortable chair he had on his first visit to the small room and recommenced his research, delving deeper into the ancient documents.

The scent of old parchment and mildew filled Richard's nostrils. Dust motes danced in the faint light that filtered through the narrow window, casting eerie shadows on the ancient documents before him. He felt a mixture of excitement and trepidation, knowing that within these records, he might find hints of the dark legacy surrounding the mysterious Rachel.

Richard carefully leafed through the brittle pages, searching for any mention of the grove or a girl named Rachel. The minutes slipped away as he scrutinised birth records, marriage registers, and accounts of deaths and burials. His back grew numb, and his eyes ached, but his determination remained unwavering.

Finally, Richard found a single entry detailing the tragic end of a young woman named Rachel, her disappearance, and the subsequent discovery of her body in the grove with no explanation for her demise. The record was vague and incomplete, but it was enough to drive him on with a sense of urgency to uncover more about this girl, her connection to the haunting voice he had heard, and, ultimately, her connection to the grove.

Thumbing through more records, Richard began to form a chilling tapestry, hinting at the dark legacy of the grove, piecing together fragments of information, each adding to a mounting sense of dread.

"Is it possible . . . ?" he wondered, his hands shaking as he turned the pages of another volume.

"If only I had more time left in here," Richard thought, "I'm sure I could find out . . ."

"Time is up, Captain Headley," the vicar announced abruptly from the doorway, startling Richard from his thoughts. "I trust you have found what you sought?"

"Almost," Richard replied, masking his frustration. "But I believe I've made progress."

"Then I suggest you focus on your work and leave our village's past where it belongs," the vicar warned, his gaze darkening. "Some stories – whether perceived as secrets, or not – are best left undisturbed."

Richard nodded, feigning compliance. But as he left St. Saviour's church, his mind raced with the pieces of the puzzle he had unearthed. The mystery of Rachel and her connection to the grove demanded more answers.

Richard knew he could no longer avoid venturing back to the cursed grove as the late afternoon sun dipped toward the horizon.

"Tonight," he whispered. "Tonight, Rachel, we will meet again . . . but on my terms."

Immediately struck by the eerie silence that blanketed the area – interrupted only by the occasional rustle of leaves in the wind – Richard found himself back at the grove again... this time all alone.

The moon cast an ethereal glow upon the clearing, casting slivers of light through the twisted branches above. Here, among these ancient trees, Richard would face the unknown.

Richard's thoughts returned momentarily to the conversation with Alfred earlier that evening, back in the warm bar of The Black Shuck Inn.

Alfred had been fearful of returning to the grove, and Richard could not blame him for that.

Despite Alfred's pleas for caution, Richard's resolve to confront the mysteries of the grove had remained unshaken, even when Alfred implored Richard not to return, making the valid point: "The things we saw last night . . . were they not enough?"

With a nod, both to his resolve to continue and also to his acknowledgement of Alfred's assistance, Richard had set off towards the grove alone, leaving Alfred and the safety of the inn behind, with his words still at the forefront of Richard's mind: "Do take care, Captain, sir."

A twig snapping underfoot broke Richard's reverie, and drawing a deep breath, he removed a bundle of candles from his satchel, each one pilfered from the inn's storeroom earlier that evening.

Placing them carefully around the perimeter of the clearing, Richard struck a match, igniting the wicks one by one, with each flickering flame pushing back the oppressive darkness, offering a small but welcome measure of solace.

As the final candle burst into life, Richard stood back and surveyed his makeshift circle of protection, the dancing flames casting eerie shadows upon the gnarled tree trunks. He knew he was treading on dangerous ground, but the quest for answers drove him onward, fuelling the determination that burned within his chest.

Summoning all his resolve, Richard stepped into the heart of the makeshift circle and began to call to the spirits that had wafted out from the cover of the mighty oaks the night before and afterwards had terrorised him at the inn. As the words spilt from his lips, an unnatural mist began to fill the grove, tendrils of fog curling around the trees like ghostly fingers. The air grew cold, colder than any earthly chill, and Richard shivered as he continued.

From the depths of the mist, whispers emerged, echoing in an unknown language through the clearing. They twisted around Richard, a cacophony of voices that defied logic and sanity. He felt the fabric of reality bending under the weight of these spectral sounds, yet he persisted, driven by a desperate need for answers.

As his throat dried up and the final syllables left his trembling mouth, the whispers ceased abruptly, leaving only an oppressive silence. The mist coalesced before him, forming the ethereal figure of a young woman. Her skin was deathly pale, her eyes hollow pits that seemed to bore into Richard's soul. A bloody gash marred her throat, a gruesome reminder of some long-ago violence.

Richard stared at the wraith before him, feeling both repulsion and a chilling fascination. She was the embodiment of the village's dark past, a spectre born from the sins and secrets that haunted this place. And while Richard's rational mind screamed at him to flee, to abandon this nightmarish encounter, another part of him could not look away. For in this ghastly apparition lay the answers he sought.

"Rachel?" he whispered hoarsely, his voice barely audible above his pounding heart. "Tell me . . . tell me that it's you."

The wraith stared back at him, her gaze cold and unfathomable. And as the candles flickered in the darkness, casting their eerie glow upon her spectral face, Richard Headley knew that he had crossed a threshold from which there was no turning back.

Richard hesitated at that liminal gate between reason and the supernatural, curiosity gnawing at him. Steeling himself, he stepped closer to the spectre. Her eyes remained locked on his, an unspoken challenge hanging in the air. He drew a shaky breath and whispered, "What do you want from me?"

The wraith's face contorted with fury, and she unleashed a deafening shriek that shook the very core of Richard's being. The sound echoed through the grove, and then, just as suddenly as she had appeared, the ghastly figure vanished into the mist.

Silence fell heavy upon the grove, but the respite was short-lived. The earth beneath Richard's feet began to tremble as if responding to the wraith's call. Hands, cold and lifeless as the grave, erupted from the ground around him, clawing at his legs with icy fingers. Terror coursed through Richard's veins as he stumbled backwards, trying to escape the clutches of the vengeful dead.

"Leave me be!" he cried, desperation tinging his voice. But the hands were relentless, pulling at him, seeking to drag him down into their dark embrace. With every ounce of strength he had left, Richard broke free, stumbling over exposed tree roots and slipping on wet leaves and twigs; he ran as he'd never run before, the weight of the ghost's reach burdening his every step.

The relentless pounding of his heart echoed in Richard's ears as he sprinted through the moonlit countryside, every nerve on edge. His breath came in ragged gasps, and the cold air stung his lungs. He could feel the icy tendrils of fear gripping him, an ever-present reminder of the spectral horrors that had pursued him from the grove.

"Are they still following me?" he thought, unable to shake the paranoia that gnawed at the edges of his mind. "Or am I being tormented by my very own demons?"

He glanced over his shoulder, half-expecting to see the spirits reaching out with bony fingers, seeking to drag him back into the darkness. But there was nothing, only the eerie silence of the night and the shadows cast by a merciless moon.

"Keep moving," he urged himself, forcing his weary limbs forward.

Finally, the familiar outline of the village emerged from the darkness and then the inn – a beacon of hope amidst the terrors that plagued him. He burst through the door, nearly collapsing from exhaustion and relief.

"Captain Headley!" the innkeeper exclaimed, startled by his dishevelled appearance. "Whatever has happened to you?"

"Just a . . ." Richard panted, struggling to catch his breath. "Just a . . . nothing really... nothing I can explain."

But deep down, Richard knew it was more than "just nothing he could explain". The night's events had left their mark on him, and he could no longer deny the existence of a malevolent force that haunted the grove on the hill above Hindringham Novers. It was a force that had seeped into the very roots of those mighty oaks and into the dark and ancient land they grew from, threatening to consume all who dared to pry into its secrets.

As he retreated to the safety of his room, Richard couldn't help but feel that the answers he sought were within reach, but so too were the vengeful spirits that guarded them.

"Rachel," he whispered, the name echoing in his mind like a lost memory. "Who are you? What do you want from me?"

The line between reality and nightmare blurred even further with each passing moment. But Richard knew he could not rest until the truth was revealed, no matter the cost. And so, with a mix of trepidation and determination, he prepared himself for whatever horrors the darkness might bring.

Chapter Eleven

When Night Holds Sway.

With a pounding heart, Richard heaved the heavy oak dresser across the floorboards of his room, its legs scraping and groaning in protest. Sweat dripped down his brow as he pushed it against the door, forming a makeshift barricade to keep out whatever malevolent force might have pursued him from the haunted grove.

Richard scanned the room with the wardrobe still protecting against entry from the window. "Let this be enough," he muttered to himself, his voice muted over his pulse pounding in his ears.

As soon as the furniture was in place, an eerie silence fell upon the room. Richard held his breath, ears straining for any sign of a spectral encroachment. Then, without warning, the door shuddered violently under the impact of a ghostly assault.

Richard recoiled, his back pressed against the rough exposed carrstone wall, as the relentless pounding continued, each blow creating a cacophony of haunting sounds reverberating throughout the room. He tried to anchor himself to his scientific background and the rational explanations he once clung to, but the terror that gripped him was too powerful to ignore.

"Leave me be . . . please leave me be," he whispered, his whole body shaking under the onslaught that seemed unending, and he could not help but wonder if his quest for knowledge had finally led him to his downfall.

Despite his fear, Richard's mind raced with thoughts of Rachel – the ghost's identity and the horrifying truth of her death. He knew he could no longer dismiss the supernatural forces at play; they were all too real, threatening not only his own life but the lives of everyone in the village.

"Rachel, I'm sorry," Richard murmured into the darkness, his breath coming in ragged gasps as he slid down the wall, his legs giving way beneath him. Exhausted and overwhelmed, he collapsed against the wooden floor, his body trembling with fear and fatigue.

His mind raced back to the church archives, where he had discovered Rachel's tragic fate – a young woman sacrificed by a sect of sinister pagans hiding in open sight within the village for centuries. The knowledge weighed heavily on him, and he felt it was now his duty to help her restless spirit find peace.

As the pounding on the door continued, Richard desperately searched the room for any semblance of safety. He found a small corner partially obscured by the heavy curtains now drawn back from the window, and he huddled there, hoping that it might offer him some protection from the malevolent forces at work.

"Stay strong," he told himself, trying to summon any remaining courage. But even as he sought comfort from his inner strength, Richard knew that the horrors he now faced were unlike anything he had encountered in his past.

In the dim light of the room, Richard could see the shadows cast by the flickering candlelight. "Please," he whispered, his voice barely audible above the sounds of the ghostly assault, "let me find a way to put this right."

But even as he uttered these words, Richard knew that to do so he would have to confront not only the horrifying truth of Rachel's sacrifice but also the insidious forces that accompanied her drifting spirit.

For now, though, he could only huddle in his corner, praying that the torment would end, and the light of day would bring some respite from the horrors that haunted him. And as he clung to this fragile hope, Richard knew that he could not – would not – give up.

The ghost's anguished wailing swirled outside the door like a haunting melody. Richard felt shivers travelling down his spine as the mournful cries echoed through the room. He couldn't shake from his mind the image of Rachel's contorted face back in the grove – a face twisted in eternal torment.

"Curse this village and its dark secrets," he muttered, pressing his trembling hands over his ears – desperate to block out the noise, trying to shut out the terrifying sounds surrounding him. Not for the first time over recent days, Richard wished he had never ventured into Hindringham Novers, never sought to uncover the mysteries that now threatened to consume him.

But he knew he couldn't turn the clock back and knew he was not a man to give in lightly. In his mind's eye, Richard saw the pages of ancient tomes filled with tales of rituals and sacrifices, the fearful villagers who refused to speak of their ancestors' deeds and the chilling records he had uncovered within the church archives. Each piece of the puzzle only strengthened his resolve, even as fear gnawed at the edges of his sanity.

With each passing hour, Richard's determination grew stronger, fuelled by the memories of his past life in academia; his studies and research often obscured by mystique and uncertainty, reminding him that his path through life had brought him here, now, to bring reason and light to this place shrouded in darkness.

The relentless pounding and wailing outside his door became a nightmarish symphony of terror. Yet, it only served to remind him of the stakes at hand – the village's safety, the truth about Rachel, and the horrifying legacy of her sacrifice.

"Please," Richard murmured, his voice barely audible. "Let this torment end."

The ghostly cries echoed through Richard's room, their mournful wails a haunting reminder of the darkness that lurked beyond. He tried to focus on his breath, steady and controlled, while the sounds outside his makeshift defences threatened to consume him – yet in the darkness, the memories of the church records and the tragic tale of Rachel filled his thoughts.

Richard clung to the hope that morning would dispel the shadows that plagued him, both literally and metaphorically. The dawn would bring clarity and a renewed determination to delve deeper into the village's hidden past. He sought comfort in believing reason and logic could prevail over fear and superstition.

As the time passed and the ghostly cries continued unabated, Richard's mind drifted again to Kings College – the confident, rational man he had been before setting foot in this accursed village. He longed for the safety of academia, the comforting embrace of knowledge and understanding.

The night wore on like a warped clock, each hour stretching longer and more torturous than the last. The pounding on Richard's door refused to cease, blending with the ghostly wails outside into an unholy symphony of dread and despair. He found himself caught between the relentless torment of the supernatural forces and the maddening rhythm of his own racing heart.

"Rachel," Richard whispered. He clung to her name as though it were a lifeline in a storm of terror – a single thread that, if pulled, could unravel the entire tapestry of the village's dark past.

Who was she? And what part did she play in this haunting tale?

Richard's thoughts swirled around the horrifying revelations he had uncovered in the church archives. He remembered the childlike voice whispering, "Let me sleep" in his mind and the ghostly figure that had appeared before him in the grove. Rachel's spirit seemed inexorably linked to the malevolent force that haunted the village and its people.

In the small hours of the night, when the shadows swallowed his room, Richard imagined the story of Rachel unfolding before his eyes. He saw her as a young girl, innocent and completely unaware of the terrible fate that awaited her.

Throughout the night, the truth had made itself known to Richard – through the voices within the wails and screams from the spectres on the other side of his flimsy barricade – embedding a growing sense of responsibility for the tortured soul that now plagued him.

Despite the horrors that continued to assault him, Richard's determination to solve the mystery of Rachel and the grove grew stronger –

he would not allow himself to be defeated by fear or superstition, for he was a man of reason, a seeker of truth.

And as the first light of dawn crept through the cracks in his barricade, Richard slumped against the wall, his heart pounding in his chest, his skin clammy with fear. The relentless assault had continued throughout the night, leaving him desperate and exhausted as he tried to cling to any semblance of rational thought, even as the haunting wails of the ghostly apparition that had pursued him continued to reverberate through the air.

"Rachel," he whispered, struggling to make sense of the horrifying truth about her cruel fate: a young girl from Hindringham Novers, taken by a group of pagans in the 17th century and sacrificed in a bloody ritual to some long-forgotten woodland deity. The malevolent force that haunted the grove had been born from that dark act, its power sustained by the villagers who continued to practice their twisted traditions generation after generation.

Richard's thoughts raced, torn between his desire for knowledge and the paralyzing fear that gripped him. Sure in his mind now that the ghostly figure was indeed Rachel herself, trapped in eternal torment and seeking vengeance upon those who had wronged her, Richard questioned what if the villagers knew more than they let on – could they, or their ancestors, be complicit in her suffering?

In a moment of desperation, Richard peered out from his hiding place, catching a glimpse of Rachel's contorted face in the shadows of the hallway. Her eyes bore into his soul, and he shuddered at her twisted, anguished expression. There was no denying it now: the darkness he sought to unveil had finally revealed itself, and its horror pressed down upon him.

He felt helpless and trapped, unable to withstand the onslaught of her anguish any longer. The room seemed to close in around him, a suffocating darkness that sought to smother his last vestiges of reason.

"Please," Richard whispered in desperation, "leave me be! I will find a way to help you, but this torment must cease."

As he retreated into the safety of his corner, Richard couldn't help but wonder if his promise was futile. How could he, a mere mortal, hope to stand against the dark forces that had held sway over the grove and the village for centuries?

Curled tight in his corner and wrapped in the heavy curtain, Richard clung to the newly arriving daylight as a child clings to a favourite toy. He thought back to the church records, the chilling accounts of rituals and sacrifices.

The spirits had revealed the truth to him and, with it, a form of respite, for there was now nothing more for him to discover, no more tragic or horrific story to be revealed. He now knew all there was to know about the curse that hung over the grove and village like a shroud.

The early dawn light filtered through the small square window-panes, driving out the darkness that had gripped the room for what had seemed to Richard like an eternity.

The shadows receded, leaving only the trembling husk of a man who had once proudly defied the superstitions of Hindringham Novers.

Chapter Twelve

Reckonings and Resolutions

B reakfast had finished, and standing in the large bay window, watching the village slowly stir into life, Richard observed how the villagers were seemingly unaffected by the dark secrets that lurked beneath the surface as they bustled about their daily routines.

Their laughter and idle chatter grated on his frayed nerves, and Richard wondered if they were genuinely ignorant of what had transpired in the grove and, latterly, at the inn or if they chose to ignore it out of fear.

"Morning, Captain," greeted the innkeeper cheerfully as he sidled up to Richard, oblivious to his internal turmoil. "Did you sleep well?"

"Ah, yes, thank you," Richard lied, forcing a smile. It was futile to divulge the horrors he had experienced; the truth would only be met with suspicion and ultimately with denial.

"Your account, Captain, sir," said the innkeeper, "I've left it in your room. If you check that everything is in order, I can send it to your people in Cambridge for settlement."

"Thank you . . . yes, of course," Richard replied. "I'll bring it down with me after I've packed."

Returning to his room, Richard immediately noticed the furniture had been moved, the wardrobe back against the wall now enabled the morning light to stream through the window.

All was how it should be. Some semblances of order had returned.

Richard picked up the small cream envelope from the bed, his name written in a neat script. Opening it, he stared at the numbers on the statement of account, not assessing the figures in great detail; the total looked like a reasonable sum for his stay, so he signed the account and slipped it back into the envelope.

Gazing out at the peaceful village below, Richard once again felt a strange mix of emotions; he knew he had confronted and faced down the entities that had invaded this room only hours before and had, in some small measure, unravelled the mysteries surrounding the grove and the village. Yet... he couldn't shake the feeling that he would never truly escape the ghosts that had haunted him – that he would forever hear the whispers of the spirits, eternally etched into his mind.

Methodically, Richard began to pack his belongings. His hands trembled as he folded his clothes and placed them into his suitcase, his mind replaying the chilling encounters over the past days. He gathered his notes, maps, and research materials and stuffed them into his Gladstone bag – ensuring nothing was left behind.

"Focus, old man," he muttered as he continued packing his belongings. The familiar act grounded him, reminding him of the man he was before he'd arrived in Hindringham Novers. "Nothing makes sense anymore," he whispered, his hands trembling as he secured the last buckle on his bag.

Downstairs, Richard approached the innkeeper and handed him the signed statement of account. They exchanged pleasantries as the innkeeper checked that his records were correct regarding whom he should forward the account to in Cambridge.

"Thank you, Captain Headley. I do hope your stay with us has been... productive," said the innkeeper.

Richard hesitated, unsure of how to respond. Did the man know about the attack on him last night? Was he complicit in the events occurring at the grove – events that affected every aspect of life in this village?

Equally, Richard couldn't help but wonder what the innkeeper thought of him, as a person. Did he see Richard as a foolish outsider meddling in things he didn't understand? Or did he recognise the resolve that burned within him, driving him to seek answers?

"Thank you," Richard managed finally, forcing a smile. "It has been . . . enlightening."

"Ah, Captain, sir," the innkeeper said, his tone cautiously warm as he returned Richard's gaze. "Your determination to unearth our village's past has certainly caused quite a stir. I trust you've found some answers to your questions?"

Richard weighed his response carefully, aware of the innkeeper's suspicion. "I've uncovered much more than I could have imagined," he admitted. "This place is steeped in history and mystery."

Although apprehensive, Richard realised that his initial assessment of the geographical position of the village hadn't altered. Regarding ease of access, the village was ideally situated for the various locations across East Anglia he would likely visit for future evaluations and surveys.

"In fact, I think it would be wise for me to return to Hindringham Novers and make The Black Shuck Inn my base of operations while continuing with my War Department duties," Richard added.

The innkeeper arched an eyebrow but nodded approvingly. "That sounds like a fine idea, sir. We'd be happy to have you stay with us again. We always aim to give our patrons a relaxing break from their hectic lives."

Richard offered a tight-lipped smile, his thoughts filled with ghostly apparitions, cryptic records, and the enigmatic figure of Rachel. "Thank you," he replied, "But my future visits will be more pressing, dictated by the threat from overseas."

"Yes... of course, sir. Good luck, Captain Headley," the innkeeper said sombrely. "We all live under shadows, not of our wanting – but perhaps there is hope that one day they can be lifted."

"Goodbye," Richard said, turning to leave the inn. He knew that whatever lay ahead, the ghosts of Hindringham Novers had laid their claim on him, and he would carry their stories with him until he found the strength to set himself free.

Richard glanced at his pocket watch, anticipating Corporal Meadows' arrival. As he reflected on the events that had transpired over recent days, he understood that he could never truly escape the village's lingering presence. He also knew that his perspective must change if he was to play his part – however small – in confronting the looming threat to Britain.

The morning sun broke through the low-lying cloud cover, casting its light upon the village square. Richard felt the warmth on his face as it began to dissolve the icy grip of fear that had held him captive throughout the night.

"Captain Headley!" a voice called out, jolting Richard back to the present moment. Squinting against the sunlight, he spotted Corporal Meadows approaching, his military uniform crisp and professional. Relief washed over Richard at the sight of a familiar face – a face unblemished by the horrors that had haunted Hindringham Novers.

"Corporal Meadows," he replied, waving him over. "Good to see you. I hope your visit to Sheringham went well."

"Likewise, sir. Yes, everything is fine there," Corporal Meadows said, his expression betraying a hint of concern. "But if you don't mind me saying so, you look like you've seen better days, sir."

"You have no idea," Richard muttered under his breath, forcing a smile onto his face. He knew he could not yet share the full extent of what he'd experienced with the corporal. Not yet . . . anyhow.

"Captain Headley, are you ready to depart?" Corporal Meadows asked as he looked at the bags by Richard's feet.

"Certainly," Richard replied, his voice betraying a hint of exhaustion.

"I've parked the car just over there . . ." the corporal pointed to the familiar shape of the Austin Seven. "Here, let me take that for you."

The corporal strolled off with the suitcase, and as Richard picked up his matching leather Gladstone bag, his gaze fell upon five deep scratches in the weathered grain. He ran his fingers over them, sure that Rachel's ghost had left her mark as a reminder that he would never truly escape her vengeance for his role in rousing her, borne of his own reckless curiosity.

Despite feeling like he had escaped the terror of the grove, Richard knew the memories of the restless dead would continue haunting him. As he closed his eyes, shivering at the thought of how close he had come to losing himself in the darkness of that place, the ghostly screams echoed once more in his mind.

"Captain?" Corporal Meadows called to him, concern evident in his tone.

"Right," Richard said, shaking off his morbid thoughts. "I'm coming."

As they drove through the village, heading for the coast road that would take them east and then onto Cambridge, Richard couldn't help but feel a renewed sense of purpose. The darkness that had consumed him was now tempered with determination and an understanding that they were still bound by a duty to protect their homeland despite the otherworldly forces that surrounded them.

Richard knew that their survey work in East Anglia had only just begun, and as the threat of German invasion grew darker, the people of this area would no doubt have to endure great privations and face their worst fears if the enemy was to be defeated.

And Richard was no exception – he had ventured here thinking to conquer isolated darkness and superstition with the light of reason and science. Still, now, for his own survival, he knew his outlook and attitude must change.

"We must never forget," Richard thought, "that even in the face of terror, we must stand strong. For it is only through courage and conviction that we can hope to overcome the darkness."

Thank you for reading my book – I really hope that you enjoyed it. Now you have finished if you have time, could you please leave a review?

You can find out more about my series of books at :

Andrew Fordham : Amazon Author Page

I really enjoy engaging with readers of my books and will be setting up a blog page on my website, where over time, I will give insights into my writing processes - such as characterisation, settings, and plot research, and will also use the Blog pages to keep readers informed of my upcoming new books and series.

I hope to see you there !

Printed in Great Britain
by Amazon